TAKING
CHANCES
A M/M NOVELLA COLLECTION

BURNING UP THE SHEETS, LLC
    23139 LAUREL WAY
    HOLLYWOOD, MD 20636

COVER DESIGN BY: SIMPLY DEFINED ART

MANUFACTURED IN THE UNITED STATES OF AMERICA
    FIRST EDITION: JUNE 2018

Taking Chances

Three sexy male/male novellas of taking chance on love . . .

GHOST

Oliver Burns knew sneaking out on the most delicious one-night-stand he ever had would come back and bite him in the ass. Caught up in his own swagger when he was named to the "30 under 30" list, he publicly bragged that his next goal was to sign the reclusive artist "G" to his talent roster at his comic publishing company and now he's got to make it happen.

SHADOW RANCH

Returning to the ranch where your mother killed your father is nobody's idea of fun but Eli Sutherland didn't have anywhere else to go. When the welcome wagon delivers a concussion and a dead body to his farm, sexy Texas Ranger Shep Lockwood is the only good thing about making the move to middle of nowhere Texas.

FREE AGENT

Defenseman James "DC" Washington has had a big year: winning "The Cup" and coming out to his team and the entire world were events that changed his life. Now a free agent, he thought he had his next step all planned out . . . until the man he might not be able to resist puts a sexy offer on the table.

GHOST

GHOST

Oliver Burns knew sneaking out on the most delicious one-night-stand he ever had would come back and bite him in the ass. Caught up in his own swagger when he was named to the "30 under 30" list, he publicly bragged that his next goal was to sign the reclusive artist "G" to his talent roster at his comic publishing company and now he's got to make it happen.

So, Oliver can only laugh when he realizes that the guy he pulled a post-sex runner on a couple of years earlier is Gareth Rain, also known as "G" – creator of the First Nations graphic novel juggernaut, Ghost Warriors – and the one man he always regretted leaving behind. But Oliver didn't get to the top by giving up, so now he's laser focused on two things: getting Gareth on his team and back in his bed.

Prologue

OLIVER

I COULD STILL FEEL his hands all over me.

Calloused. Broad. Long, ink-stained, sexy fingers that I'd wanted wrapped around my dick from the first moment I'd spotted him drawing on the con floor.

They'd felt even better in real life. Slick with spit, lube, and pre-cum and tight on me while he ordered me not to shoot. He'd made it worth the wait.

Damn. I really wanted to get back in that bed.

The guy, Gareth, was sprawled on the massive bed of his hotel room, long, muscular legs wrapped up in the twist of the few sheets remaining on the mattress, the rest of the bedding strewn all over the floor with condom wrappers and empty bottles of booze from the mini-bar. The room was trashed in that   let's-fuck-and-be-as-dirty-as-we-want-because-this-is-never-gonna-happen-again way that makes you glad you aren't going to see the housekeeper ever again. My freshly-fucked ass clenched in anticipation as I recalled just how many ways he'd taken me and how I'd given in to this particular sexy fucker.

At twenty years old and several years younger than me, he wasn't anything like the older men I usually took to my bed. But there was something about his eyes, his soul that spoke of years of living his flesh did not disclose. Quiet and intense, he'd captured my attention and my interest and, like most things in my life, I didn't give up until I had him.

His copper skin was darker in the low light of the pre-dawn morning that broke through the places where the curtains didn't quite meet. Shadows contoured the dips of his muscles and obscured the beauty of his body. I wanted to turn on the light and get a better look, a closer look, a look that I would burn on my brain like it was a brand on skin. His tattoos, too many to count, played peek-a-boo with me through the waist-length fall of his ink-black hair and I remembered the taste of them on my tongue.

As cliché as it sounded, his hair was like silk on my skin, wrapping itself around me as we tumbled together on the sheets. I fucking loved his hair, had confessed it against the sweat-slick of his skin sometime in the darkest hours of the night and refused to be ashamed of it now. The light of day might make me rethink the booze but I wouldn't feel bad about taking this boy to my bed.

I also wouldn't acknowledge the regret pricking at my mind over leaving Gareth behind. I wanted to stay.

I never wanted to stay.

I wouldn't leave a number.

I wouldn't make plans to do this again.

I would walk out of this room and get back to what I needed to do. To build my company and prove that I could do this on my own.

So, I did what I did best.

I left.

Oliver

Three years later.
The George Peabody Library, Baltimore, MD

"They have a robe for you to wear, you know."

I looked over at Ellis and down at the fluffy, white robe she dangled from her fingertips and thrust in my direction. It looked comfortable, lush, and very warm. I didn't need it. I wasn't cold and nudity was never an issue for me

The library space where we stood soared upward six stories to the most majestic and intricately paned skylight I'd ever seen. A testament to neo-Greco architecture, the ornamental black, cast iron balconies and gold-scalloped columns testified as to why the 140-year old building was one of the most beautiful in the world and why the 30 Under 30 people had chosen it for my film location. The crew for the "Hot Naked Guys Reading" charity calendar shoot was bustling around us, moving equipment and props for the next set of photographs. I'd been here for a couple of hours already, doing my part for charity by posing naked . . . while reading. Hotly. As you do.

"I'm good, thanks," I said, grinning at the inevitable flip of her bottle green hair off her face so that I could receive the full brunt of her oh-so-dramatic eye roll. My best friend since college, former lover, and business partner was annoyed with me. And since it was her self-appointed task to attempt to keep me in some sort of line with the rest of society, this mood was one she spent of a lot time experiencing.

One day she'd realize that keeping me in check was a fruitless endeavor but I hoped it wasn't too soon. It was my singular joy to bug the shit out of her at every opportunity.

"Yeah, I'm sure you are but nobody here wants to spend all day staring at your somewhat impressive junk."

That deserved the glare I nailed her with, my gaze set to stun but just a hair's breadth from death ray.

"Somewhat impressive? What the . . ." I sputtered with genuine shock at the turn this conversation had taken, gathering my thoughts and gesturing at the insulted piece of my anatomy with a pointed sweep of my hand. "What the fuck, El? I remember you being quite impressed with it at one time."

I ignored the stares of the few makeup, lighting and random people standing nearby us. It was no secret that Ellis Walsh and I had started out as lovers, the now-famous article of how we'd practiced an open relationship for several years had made more people privy to our sex lives than was really necessary. Bi-sexual geeks who loved comic books and now co-owned the fastest growing indie comic and graphic novel publishing company in the country – we'd never given a shit about what anyone else thought as long as we had each other. Epic Publishing was our baby, brought to life through long hours and hard work.

So, this . . . cold betrayal chapped my ass.

"Oli, you're a grower, not a shower," Ellis bit back the laugh I could see crinkling at the edges of her eyes. I grabbed for her but she shoved the robe at me again and I had no choice but to grab it and prevent it from hitting the ground.

"Put that on. Your body is delicious but these people are trying to work."

"It's a naked photo shoot. If they didn't expect to see a penis then they showed up the wrong day for work."

"Just put the damn robe on and talk to me about this amazing information you've been hinting at all morning."

"You just wait until it's your turn next month." I slid the robe on, loosely tying the belt around my waist. "Hot Naked Gals Reading . . ."

She waved me off, her cheeks pinking up under her makeup. Ellis was my no-holds-barred feminist and badass but that didn't equal dropping her drawers in front of a roomful of strangers. El was the calm to my storm, the head to my heart and I'd been shocked when she'd agreed to the photoshoot. But, being named as one of the 30 Under 30 up-and-coming entrepreneurs in the country was huge and when they asked you to participate in a charity calendar, you really couldn't say no.

My phone ringing stopped me from relaying to her my juicy insider info but a quick glance at the Caller ID made me smile and put the call on speaker phone.

"Dave, what's up?"

Ellis glanced down at the display and her gaze shot back to mine when she read the name of Dave Price, the owner and publisher at Allied Comics. Dave was a colleague, not really a friend and always our fiercest competitor for talent and reader-ship. Who the fuck knew what he wanted.

"Oliver, where are you?"

I grinned at his frazzled tone, settling in for what could be a fun phone call. "Why? You want to send me an Edible Arrangement?"

"Unless they also deliver *me* kicking *your ass*, then fuck no." He didn't even pause long enough for me to reply, charging on in his Boston-accent-laced bellow. "Oliver, did

5

you tank the deal "G" had with me? What the fuck did you do?"

El's gaze shot to join mine as we both leaned in closer to the phone, our bodies mirroring each other in our laser-focused concentration.

"Dave, did you lose your new artist?" Ellis reached out and touched my arm in caution, but I couldn't have removed the teasing scorn from my voice even if I'd wanted to. But I didn't want to. This news was pretty much the best thing I'd heard all year. "This is why we can't have nice things."

"Oliver, I don't know what you did . . ."

"I didn't do anything Dave, but I'd love to know what *you* did so that I don't make the same mistake." I evened out my tone, adding enough sincere interest to hopefully get some good info. "I swear to God Dave, I didn't do anything because I thought you had him on lock. Papers signed. What happened?"

Silence. Nothing from the other end of the line and I looked at Ellis. She shook her head, leaning closer to the phone as a long, frustrated sigh slithered out from the speaker.

"I don't know. I figured you'd lured him away with your flashy West Coast daddy's money bullshit," he said and I let it go but my verbal restraint didn't stop the flush of anger creeping up my neck. Ellis reached out again and this time she squeezed my arm and shook her head in warning.

"Dave, I never got past his agent, Neal Woodson." I answered, opting for honesty even if was talking to the enemy. "You know how G is. Reclusive. Secretive."

"It's like he's fucking Batman."

"And now he's free agent Batman."

A bigger sigh and then steel in his voice. "If you fucked me over, Oliver . . ."

"I didn't but if I had . . . it's business Dave. Nothing personal." I paused and stared at Ellis, letting the grin pushing at my lips take over. She narrowed her eyes at me. "And it will be nothing personal when I sign him with us."

"I don't even think your particular brand of fast talk and bullshit could get him to sign with you. What are you gonna do? Throw some of your family money at him?"

He'd thrown down the red flag in front of me. Again. Game on.

"You wanna bet?"

Ellis whipped her head up so fast I felt it crack the bones in *my* neck. Ouch. She started shaking her head, the emphatic effort to get me to stop where this was going making her green curls whip around her face. It was cute. Useless but cute. We all knew where this was going.

Dave was already there. "Sure. Let's do that."

"Wager?"

"Five grand."

Ellis reeled backwards, her arms flailing around her body in the universal signal for "have you lost your fucking mind?" I ignored her.

"Deal. Winner coughs up five grand," I couldn't resist getting in a final dig. "I'll give G your money as a signing bonus."

"Fuck you, Oliver."

"Right back at ya." I swiped over the screen of the phone and looked at Ellis, my grin widening as I realized the full extent of this new development. "We're going to sign G to our roster." I reached out and grabbed her by the shoulders and shook her lightly. "Fucking G, Ellis!"

"Oliver, we're booked here at the comic con for the next few days. When do you think you're going to have time to find G and convince him to meet you and sign him to Epic?

"He's here. In Baltimore. At the con." I tossed the phone up into the air and caught it, sliding it into the pocket of my robe with a flourish.

"You know where he is?"

What did she think I was? An amateur?

"I've been borderline stalking the guy for the last year. Of course, I know where is."

"G doesn't do conventions"

"True but he's doing a charity signing here tomorrow to kick off the indigenous comic event here at the convention. One afternoon. Here in Baltimore. I've got VIP passes. I paid out the ass for them."

I loved watching her expression morph from confusion, to disbelief, to admiration tinged with anger. This is why we'd never worked as a couple: there wasn't enough makeup sex in the world to fix how pissed she was at me most of the time.

"When were you going to tell me about this stunt," she asked, her lips sill pulled into a mulishly pissed line.

"Honestly? Tomorrow. I was going to surprise you with the passes," I answered, knowing that wasn't what she was asking. She knew me better than anyone else on the planet and the fact that she still loved me anyway was a miracle. I'm not easy to love so I tried to give her honesty. "I was going to make a play for him to sign with us no matter what. Contracts were made to be broken. Dave's call just gave me hope that we might have a chance."

Ellis snorted, crossing her arms across her chest in irritation. I wasn't off the hook yet. "So, the bet? What the hell was that?" She pointed at me. "That's not coming out of Epic funds, Oliver. You lose, *you pay*."

"I'm not going to lose. G wouldn't have gotten so close to signing with Allied if he wasn't looking for a deal. All I need is a little bit of time with him to convince him that we're obviously the best fucking choice."

"Just a little time, huh?" Ellis was skeptical, justifiably so. "G has dodged every single phone call we've made to his management, Oliver. Not even a meeting. It's been so complete that it's starting to feel personal and you think you can seal a deal with a little bit of time? Not even you're that good."

Now that stung worse than the crack about my dick size. "Ellis, I always get what I want. I'll get G."

"How was it that reporter described you?" Ellis cocked her head at me, her expression a blend of admiration and admonition. "Humble with a hint of Kanye?

I grinned. "Yeah, well, humility is overrated."

Gareth

I looked down at my trembling fingers and cursed.

Neal sidled up closer to me and peered down onto the hand I was clenching and unclenching in an attempt to stop the shaking. It wasn't that it hadn't happened before. I had an essential tremor so it happened all the time. I just didn't want it to happen now.

"I thought the new meds were working," Neal said, his eyes on my face and no longer on the fist I was making over and over. He knew staring only made me more self-conscious and the more self-conscious I became the worse the tremor would get. "Do we need to get back with your doctor?"

"No. The meds are good," I answered, solving the problem by shoving the unruly appendage into my jeans pocket. "I'm just nervous."

"I think I told you how proud I am of you, Gareth. I know you hate this kind of stuff."

I did, but hate wasn't the accurate word. It was fear. I was terrified of stuff like this. I didn't like the attention, the eyes on me, the need to constantly make small talk with strangers. All of that stuff made me want to puke. I'd had my eye on the restroom since we'd arrived at the convention hall an hour ago.

"Hank caught me in a moment of weakness," I unnecessarily explained again to Neal. He'd heard it all before but talking to him was getting my mind off my hand shaking. "The LGBTQIA teen shelter needed money to add on a soup kitchen and I promised to help him raise the funds."

"Was that moment of weakness while in his bed or at the bar?" Neal inquired, his lips sliding into the mischievous grin that completely changed his craggy, rugged face into something infinitely more approachable. A mountain of a man, he was one of the few men who dwarfed me and his size and demeanor had intimidated me when we first met. Now, I was glad he scared most people at first sight and served as a buffer between me and the rest of the world.

"Hank hasn't tapped me for a booty call in over a year." I offered, shrugging when Neal gave me the "I'm getting laid on the regular so I'm very sad for you" shoulder shrug. He was in love with Callie and they still couldn't keep their hands off each other after three years together. They had that thing that hit like a lightning strike in real life and on the page of my comics. "It's for a good cause and that's important to me."

He nodded, glancing around as the convention staff rushed around with last minute preparation. "I'll be here the whole time, so just signal if you need a break or a save." Neal paused from whatever he was going to do and leaned in close. "Look, it's out that the deal fell through with Allied so publishers will be ready to pitch to you once they know you're here. I'll run interference as much as I can but . . ."

"You can't be with me everywhere."

He nodded, lifting a hand to gesture at my face. "And now that they'll know who you are . . . it's going to be harder to shield you from all of . . ." He moved his hand to encompass everyone around us. ". . . all of them."

I knew this. I'd known it when I'd accepted the invitation for this signing. This was the second coming out of my life and this one seemed more important and scarier. But I had my reasons. Important ones.

"I got it. People. I might have to talk to them and say no. Multiple times. Got it."

"We can still find you a deal." I cut him a look and he raised his hands up in a "don't shoot the messenger" gesture. "One that you can live with."

"No more liars, Neal. No more hidden agendas and I keep creative control. I need to make the money. I don't think that's so hard."

"It's not. We'll figure it out." He glanced down at his watch when a lady wearing the convention shirt and carrying a clipboard and the weight of the world on her shoulders approached us. "I think it's time."

I nodded, removing my hands from my pockets and giving them both a few, tentative squeezes. The fucking tremor was still there but it was weaker. I just hoped it stayed that way for the next couple of hours. I followed the convention lady to the signing area, the buzz of voices getting louder as we got closer. My pace slowed down and Neal gave me an inquiring look but I ignored it and forced my feet to keep going.

My escort pushed back the curtain and bright lights blazed in front of me, so bright I had to raise a hand to shield my eyes until they adjusted and I could see where to walk. I wasn't really into tripping and landing on my ass in front of whoever had actually shown up.

I blinked and a wave of noise hit me. Applause, people shouting my name and more flashes of light to keep me off balance. The convention lady put a hand on my arm to steady me and while I normally didn't like being touched by random people, I was grateful for her firm guide to the table and my chair and even more grateful when I lowered myself into it.

I sat there for a few moments, getting my bearings as people continued to snap photos but the noise of the crowd lessened as the minutes clicked by. The lull was worse than the noise since I could now see the crowd of people, the line of people filling the space and starting at me.

"You okay?" Neal's whisper in my ear startled me but I managed to not jump like the boogeyman had sprung up beside me.

"What the fuck are they all staring at?" I asked him, reaching out to grab a pen off the table for the lack of anything else to do with my hands. I always felt better, grounded, with a pen in my hands.

"They're staring at G. They've never seen him before."

Oh that. I kept forgetting about the great unveiling of my secret identity.

"Why did I agree to do this again?"

"You told me it was for the kids," Neal replied, patting me on the shoulder before he stepped back and let the convention lady make my introduction.

"Welcome to the charity book signing for the Safe Harbor Teen Shelter. I can't express to you how grateful we are that you bought tickets to support this event and this great cause but we're most grateful to Gareth Rain, also known to all of you as G. His web comic, Ghost Warriors, is a worldwide sensation, an "own voices" graphic novel juggernaut that has taken the world of comics by storm. We are so pleased that today, at this event, Mr. Rain has decided to step out from behind his drawings to show his face to the world."

The crowd started up again with the applause and I wanted to sink behind the convenient shield of my hair. Or into the floor. Either one would be fine. I scanned the mass of faces, searching for some focal point to latch onto. I let my gaze wander until I saw a face I knew, one from a night a few years ago. A face I'd never forgotten.

Oliver Burns.

Of course, I'd never forgotten what he looked like. I'd never had the chance to forget. His gorgeous, finely-boned, arrogant face was plastered all over the internet, magazines, and TMZ. Independent publishing's out-and-proud rich boy who stopped at nothing to get what he wanted and usually succeeded. The man who'd spent the night with me and then left like a john who had to get back to the wife and kids in the suburbs. He'd left my wallet but taken something with him I'd never named and he never gave back.

The guy I'd never stopped wanting.

The man who was staring at me like he'd seen a ghost.

I smiled at the irony of the moment and broke eye contact with him just as the first person approached to have me sign, chat and pose for a picture. One after another, an unending line of people all anxious to tell me how much they loved Ghost Warriors, how it had impacted their lives, how they felt like we were best friends or something. Some of them, a lot of them, cried and that freaked me the hell out.

But nothing was weirder than watching Oliver watch me from across the room. He tracked me like a dog on the trail of an escaped convict and it took everything in me to concentrate on the fans and block him out.

I knew exactly when his posture changed and his body angled towards me with his intent to approach. My whole body responded to his movement, skin and nerves tingling like an electric current was zinging across the rapidly closing space between us. My right hand shook, the pen tapping against the tabletop with the music of my disability and nerves. I slipped it under the surface as he eased in front of me, his grin wide.

"Hello again," he said, placing a palm on the table and angling his body towards me. His smile stuttered for a second and I wondered if he remembered that this was how we'd begun three years ago. Him approaching my table and acting as if we'd known each other forever.

The weirdest part was that it was exactly how it had felt between us from the beginning.

Damn it. It still felt that way.

"I don't remember us saying goodbye," I said, my voice a hell of lot calmer than I was feeling at the moment.

"What?" His eyes narrowed in confusion behind his glasses.

"You need to say goodbye before you can say hello again, Oli." I reached over and grabbed a copy of the comic to sign for him. "The last time I saw you, you didn't bother to stick around long enough to say goodbye."

I dipped my head down, allowing my hair to block out part of my face from his gaze. The silence lengthened between us and I let it go. Having to fill the gap between words was not something I had to do. I'm very content with the quiet. My closest friends have always existed in my head and they don't require a lot of conversation.

Oli was a talker. He couldn't help himself.

"So, we're still pissed about that?"

"I'm not mad. I'm just stating the facts."

I finished my autograph, closed the cover of the book and slid it across the table towards him. My hand trembled and I pulled it back and placed it in my lap once again. I lifted my gaze to look at him and found his eyes on the spot where my hand was out of sight. Too bad he didn't have x-ray vision like one of my characters.

I watched him as he slowly broke his concentration and met my gaze once again. I'd thrown the legendary Oliver Burns off his game and I took a lot of satisfaction from that. I wasn't the almost-boy he'd seduced, fucked, and left to wake up in a hotel room alone.

I nodded towards the book. "Don't forget your copy. It's a limited edition."

Oli hesitated for a moment, pausing to scour my face for clues of how to turn this thing back to where he'd planned for this to go. I could see the calculations and next steps being mapped out in his brain and I also saw the moment when he decided that now was not his time and today was not his day. He reached down and ran his fingers over the cover of the comic book and I reacted with a slight shiver, remembering how it had felt to have him trace them over my body and in my hair. He'd loved my hair.

Oli picked up the book and read the inscription, his eyes narrowed again when he looked at me. "$263.22? What is that?"

I looked beyond him and motioned for the goth chick standing behind him to move forward. "It's the amount of the mini-bar bill you stuck me with."

Oliver

"I don't know what's going to get you in more trouble, your dick or your mouth."

I flipped Ellis the bird, keeping my eyes on Gareth. I'd have known him anywhere. It was the hair, waist-length and the deepest black and laced with threads of russet. I'd wanted to touch it, to coax that smile out of him that had grabbed me from the first time I'd told him how much I liked his work.

Not today. He was still pissed.

"You know that this significantly diminishes your chances of winning your bet," Ellis continued, her finger poking into my side as she pointed out the fucking obvious. But I never gave up that easily, she knew this.

"I can fix this."

"How? You stiffed him with a mini-bar bill after you picked him up at a convention and fucked him."

"He topped, actually."

Ellis growled under her breath and several people turned to look at her and then shifted away. Smart people.

"Oliver, one more stupid comment and I'm going to kick

your ass." She shifted so that she blocked my view of Gareth. "Why didn't you ever tell me you slept with G?"

"Because until a couple of hours ago, I only knew that I'd slept with a 20 year old Cree guy from Montana who drew amazing graphics. I had no idea that he was G. Hell, *nobody* knew who G was until a little while ago."

"So, what are you going to do about it? Do you think I should take over the approach for Epic?"

"What? No. I got this."

"Oliver, you don't have this," Ellis said, shoulders hunched with the stress of the moment. She didn't find this part fun, the signing of the artists. She was the organization partner, the brilliant numbers person. She was what kept me from going too far, spending us into bankruptcy, pissing off the investors. I wasn't going to saddle Ellis with fixing this mess. It was my mess.

"I've got this, El." I reached up and shifted her around so that she was facing Gareth. He glanced over in our direction and our eyes locked for the briefest of seconds but I felt it and so did she. Her body flexed under my hands and she sucked in a sharp breath. "That guy . . . we had a connection from the first time we met. We connected over the art, the story. His story. It's still there and I can get through to him."

She let out the breath she was holding on a long, annoyed sigh. "Oliver, please don't think that another night or two with your magic dick is going to fix this and get this guy to sign with Epic." She turned her head to look at me, her face pinched with atypical worry. "I don't think sex and fast talk can fix this."

Man, her lack of confidence hurt but not enough to stop me. I'd declared my intentions and wagered five-thousand dollars on it. But most importantly, it was that fact that G was Gareth. He was the only lover I'd ever regretted leaving behind. Even when my sexual relationship with Ellis had ended, it had been the right thing for both of us at the right time. There had been no regret. But Gareth . . . he'd possessed something that had made me feel some kind of way and that sensation had pushed me out of the door of that hotel room faster than my almost pathological need to succeed.

No, Gareth was different. In more ways than I'd even realized at the time.

I turned to Ellis and gave her a reassuring kiss on the cheek. "Let me go do my job and you do yours. I'll have him signed before the convention is over."

I scanned the room and found the guy I needed to talk to so I headed over the opposite end of the signing room. A large man, Neal Woodson was an easy man to find in most rooms but his location of watchful sentry just the right of Gareth made him stand out in the crowd of people still clamoring for G's attention.

I was more interested in getting the attention of G's gate-keeper. Nobody got to him unless they went through Neal and while I'd been rebuffed numerous times before, I wasn't good at taking no for an answer.

"Neal, I need you to arrange a meeting with Gareth for me so we can talk about how Epic can give him unparalleled distribution and support for this work," I said, pitching my voice low.

He swiveled to face me, his eyes narrowed and dark with distrust. "I can't wait to hear how you know his real name."

Oh. That.

"Three years ago we . . ." I scoured my mind for the right words to describe what had happened between us. If I said we hooked up, that wasn't even close to what it had really been. In the end, I didn't have to figure out what to call our one night together.

"Oh hell, I don't need to hear the details." He dismissed me with a wave of his hand and the shifting of his body back towards his client. "But I will say that Gareth's adamant refusal to meet with you before makes a lot more sense now." Neal cut me a look that told me he wasn't a fan of Oliver Burns. "He's not gonna meet with you."

I grinned. "I know the deal with Allied fell through. I just want the shot to tell him what Epic can offer."

Neal looked back towards Gareth, clearly weighing his options. I knew he didn't like me but I also knew that he was a professional agent and an honorable man. I wasn't above picking at his soft spots.

"Look, Neal, I'm not going to bullshit you and tell you that signing G wouldn't be a huge bonus but from what I hear he needs us too. We can offer him things he can't get for himself right now like worldwide distribution and a company to help with the logistics so that he can create. I know he's looking and all I want is a chance to lay my deal out on the table."

Neal didn't look at me while he chewed on what I said. I took the time to check out Gareth again. His hair was amazing still, long and black as night, it fell over his shoulder as he leaned in to sign a book for a fan. I let my eyes travel over his body and it was obvious that he'd filled out his large frame over the past three years. Gone was any of the softened edges of the guy barely out of his teens and what remained was all sharp angles over bronze skin and solid muscle stretching the confines of his black t-shirt.

He was delicious and captivating. His shy smile was enough to make my blood sing but it was his hands that drew my gaze and trapped it like a magnet. His hands were large, well-shaped with long tapered fingers that brought entire worlds to life on the page. I'd read every issue of GHOST WARRIORS and what he'd created was unique and powerful and spoke with a voice I'd never heard before and I'd grown up devouring comics in every shape and form.

I wanted him on my roster and if I was honest with myself,

I wanted him back in my bed. I'd never had to suffer an empty bed if I didn't want to but Gareth had been different, memorable, and I'd never forgotten him.

I continued to observe Gareth, waiting Neal out while he pondered my proposition. He was warming up to the task, adding longer and longer pieces of conversation as he signed the book. His smile was still only a hint on his full lips but his eyes sparked with humor and interest as he handed the book back to the fan.

His arm was suspended between them and for the few moments it hovered there I noticed the tremor. It was noticeable and exactly what I thought I'd glimpsed earlier.

He was shaking.

And I didn't think it was nerves.

"Oliver, let me talk to Gareth and get back to you on the meeting." Neal interrupted my observations and the split second I took my eyes off Gareth, I lost sight of the tremor. I filed it away, determined to get to the bottom of that mystery later. In this moment, Neal was keeping the door open for me to get a chance to talk to Gareth. "Are you in town for the rest of the convention?"

"Yeah, just give me a call." I nodded as he pushed himself off the wall started walking towards the backstage area of the room. "You sticking around here or going back to Montana?"

"Gareth is staying so I'm staying."

I watched him walk away, his long stride making it a quick trip to the restricted area of the space. But I didn't need to follow him and I didn't need to wait for him to call because he'd given me a key piece of information: Gareth was staying for the convention.

So, that meant I had lots of time to maneuver my own meeting with the mysterious G, get him signed with Epic, win the bet, and make-up for pulling a post-sex runner on the guy I never forgot.

Gareth

St. Nick's was my favorite bar in the world.

That was a lot considering that for as long as I could remember a bar was just the place where my old man went to get drunk and then come home and ignore me if I was lucky. So, I wasn't a fan of bars as a rule but this place was different. Maybe it was because it was located in an old church. Or maybe it was because it was owned by a former thief and the hot, ginger, bear of man standing across the bar from me.

Hank Edwards was hot, handsome in the way that only a man who was totally confident in his place in the world could be. Our affair had been like the fireworks on the 4th of July: hot, explosive and over before the sweat had died on our skin.

And looking at him now I wondered if I had a type. Older. Brash. Confident.

Sounded like someone else I knew.

"I heard the signing was a huge success Gareth," Hank said, leaning over to attach the keg to the tap. "I can't thank you enough for doing it for the shelter."

"I did it because you asked me to," I dropped my gaze and

focused on the condensation sliding down the side of my glass. "The shelter is a great place."

"Was it as bad as you thought it would? Unveiling your alter ego and talking to *all those people?*" Hank grinned, his eyebrows lifted in mock alarm.

I hated being the center of attention. It was why being G had been so easy to slip into and so hard to expose. I squeezed my hands, the tremor milder now that I wasn't under the stress of the signing.

"Fuck you. You know I don't like crowds."

"But you had them all eating out of the palm of your hand. You looked like a natural."

I stalled midway in lifting my glass to my mouth, placing it back on the bar top before I swiveled in my seat and found Oliver Burns standing in my favorite bar.

"Are you stalking me?"

Oliver grinned and slid onto the barstool next to me, completely unfazed by my reaction. I had no idea how he got here or, more importantly, he found me.

"Oli, don't make me call the cops on you," I looked at Hank. "Does your badge still work?"

"Afraid not," Hank answered, completely missing my telepathic plea to help me get this guy out of here. There were only two reasons he was here and neither of them were good for me to indulge in. "My badge lost its magic a while ago." He motioned towards the taps for Oliver. "I can, however, get you something to drink."

"Give me whatever you'd drink," Oliver said and turned back to me, his smile even wider. "To answer your question, I totally followed you here."

I glared at Hank as he served up the beer to the enemy. Well, maybe not an enemy but not a friend either. "Like I said: stalker."

"It wasn't easy. I almost lost you when you took the ferry

over here from the Inner Harbor. I've never been to Fell's Point before. It's pretty cool. The cobblestone streets and rowhouses are amazing."

I ignored him and slid off my seat, grabbing my beer to head over to my favorite booth to eat in peace and quiet.

"I'll have Sid bring your food to you when it's ready. You want me to put it in your tab?" Hank asked me, his eyes narrowed as he watched the interaction between the two of us. He was calculating just how pissed I was at this stranger and if physically evicting him from the premises was going to be necessary.

"No," I motioned towards Oliver. "He's paying. He owes me money for the mini-bar."

Oliver's laugh followed me over to the half-circle booth and I felt his warmth slither over my skin as he slid in behind me. He was a little too close for my comfort or equilibrium but I didn't scoot over. I might be rattled by his appearance in my bar but I wasn't going to let him know it.

We both settled back against the leather seat and eyeballed each other. Oliver hadn't changed much over the last three years or maybe I thought that because I'd seen him plastered all over social media and any article in any magazine that had to do with comics publishing. Oliver and his partner Ellis were all kinds of successful and breaking the balls of anyone who got in their way.

"So, are you really pissed off about the mini-bar tab?" He asked, his grin sly and his dark eyes lit up with the mischief that coated his words. He didn't feel bad about it, he just wanted to poke the bear.

"I was a poor college kid. It was a shitty thing to do."

"Agreed." He leaned over close enough for his breath to skate across my cheek. My eyes fluttered shut for the briefest moment when I caught the scent of his cologne and the warmer spice of Oliver. When I opened them again, he was staring at me, his gaze hungry and impossible to break.

The thud of a plate of cheese and bacon smothered fries and my hamburger broke the tension-filled deadlock between us. I blinked up at Hank, his frown blowing away the lingering cobwebs of desire wrapped around my brain. Oliver was a bad idea for me. I was a relationship guy, somebody who didn't jump from bed-to-bed and by my own experience and all accounts in the media, Oliver had a revolving door installed in his bedroom.

He. Was. A. Bad. Idea.

"You want another ginger ale?" Hank asked me, nodding towards the three-quarters full glass in front of me.

"Nope. I'm good," I said.

"How about you?" Hank's tone was noticeably flatter when he turned his attention to Oliver.

"I'll take another one of these. It's excellent. Good choice," Oliver responded, lifting the glass in a semi-salute. He was rewarded with a grunt and an even darker glare before he stalked back over to the bar. "Boyfriend?"

It took me a minute to realize that Oliver was talking to me. "Hank? Uh, no. Not my boyfriend."

"You two slept together." It wasn't a question.

"Shut up and eat a fry." I reached out and snagged one for me and nudged the plate in his direction. Maybe food would get him to stop talking and asking questions I didn't want to answer.

Oliver took me up on my offer and several moments passed in silence. He moaned and groaned over the cheesy, bacony goodness and I took a drink to hide the smile that tugged at my lips in spite of wanting to stay angry with him. He was unpredictable and mesmerizing and it was no big secret why I'd wanted him the minute he'd leaned over my table on the convention floor and purred, "I love your work."

"Why are you here Oliver? And don't tell me it's because you suddenly feel bad about sneaking out on me and have this undeniable need to grovel at my feet."

"Come on, I *am* sorry about that," he said, snagging another fry. "I'm groveling on the inside."

"You're such an ass."

"I am." But he didn't sound sorry. He sounded smug as hell.

"You suck at apologizing." I paused as Sid brought fresh drinks to our table, placing the glass I didn't ask for in front of me. "Pick another topic."

I realized too late that I'd opened the door and he wasn't going to just saunter in, he was going to march with a damn parade. He didn't disappoint.

"Okay, let's talk about why you should sign with Epic," he scooted close enough for our arms to brush against each other, his voice dropping down to deeper timbre, the kind that got you in his bed or on his payroll. "We can make you huge, Gareth."

Oliver's dark hair fell across his forehead and I picked up my glass so that I wouldn't reach up and sweep it back in place. But I couldn't stop the flash of memory, me taking off his glasses and placing them on bedside table before tangling my fingers in his hair to hold him in place as I tasted his kiss.

We were polar opposites until we'd fallen into bed. Then we'd been in sync, what we needed and what we could give fitting together like a puzzle. It had been easier than it ever should have been between strangers.

But his words drove home that outside the bedroom we didn't see the world the same way.

"New topic," I said.

Oliver's grin faltered a little bit for the first time since he'd walked up to my table at the signing. Apparently, he thought I was a slam dunk but I wasn't the young twenty-year old he'd dazzled three years ago.

"Gareth, I know you're looking for a publisher to partner with. Why not Epic?"

"New topic, Oliver."

He huffed out his frustration, shifting out of my personal space, arms spread across the back of the booth. I admired his ability to exude confidence even when he clearly wasn't feeling it 100%.

"So, what can we talk about? This is going to be a long date if every topic is off-limits."

Now it was my turn to do a double take. He'd lost his mind or I needed to get my hearing checked.

"A what?"

He grinned, the prince back on top of his throne. The sexy bastard. "I'm paying. We're sharing a meal. I call that a date."

Oliver

I loved surprising Gareth.

Even in the dim light of the booth I could see the blush creep along his cheekbone and I wanted to reach out feel the heat of it on my fingertips. He kept everything on such tight lockdown that I found myself living for the moments where I could get a glimpse of him beneath the armor. Making him laugh had been the unexpected delight of our night together. It wasn't a frequent occurrence so pulling one out of him felt like winning the lottery,

And tonight I really wanted to feel it again.

"A date." I pushed my glasses up on my nose and motioned between us. "You're right about my being an ass last time. Let me make it up to you. We can eat, talk." I leaned over to eyeball the dance floor. "We can dance."

He considered me across the booth, dark eyes wary but sparked with interest. There was a connection between us and I could see Gareth struggling against it, muscles clenched and rippling under his skin. I held my breath, waiting to see if he would take the leap.

"I don't dance," he answered, tone so low that I had to shift forward and lean closer to catch it. He took a breath and drove home his next point with a tap of a long finger on the table. "I don't want to talk publishing contracts with you. If you take some time to think about it, you'll admit that I'm not a good fit for Allied."

I held up my hands in surrender. If he was digging in like this then I had a clear signal that now was not the time to get him to sign. He needed time and I could give it to him because I also knew that if I played this right tonight, then I'd get my shot later. I'd get the artist and I'd win the bet. Everybody would win.

Mercenary? I didn't think so. My attraction and enjoyment of Gareth wasn't fake. I did like him and I'd let him take me to bed right now if he wanted. But business was always better when the parties could stand each other and best when they liked each other.

Honey was always better to attract bees and reclusive artists.

And we both loved a certain kind of honey.

"Cool. No shop talk tonight but am I allowed to tell you that I fucking love GHOST WARRIORS? I feel like I should have known it was yours. The story, the drawings. Now that I know it's just so obvious that you wrote it!"

I balled my hands into fists and shook them over my head, as if cursing the gods for letting me be so blind. I should have figured it out, his work had grabbed me from the beginning. And when I'd first logged onto his website to read an independent webcomic that was getting a shit ton of buzz I'd spent the entire time reminding myself to breathe.

Gareth was unique. One of a kind.

"Thanks." He dipped his head but not before I saw the flash of a grin on his lips. "It means a lot to me."

I slid across the seat, edging in close to catch every soft spoken word and lured into his personal space by the warmth of his body. He was enticing to me, irresistible and I wasn't a man who denied himself much of what he wanted.

"Such a crazy fresh twist on the whole superhero story. Warriors empowered by their ancestors and led by a two-spirit ghost. Where did you get the idea for it?

His hair brushed against the skin of my arm when he looked up to meet my gaze and a shiver slithered across my skin and settled as heat in my groin. Gareth was sexy as fuck and he didn't even know it.

"Being a kid wasn't great for me. I was gay, my family was a mess and when I was taken away from my dad and the Rocky Boy Indian Reservation in Montana they placed me in an orphanage. Nothing about my life felt safe or okay so I made up imaginary friends to help me." He shrugged and reached for his glass. "The Ghost Warriors were my friends. They helped me survive."

"And you created the webcomic to help other kids?" I thought I already knew the answer. Putting two and two together now that I knew he was G was a lot easier equation.

"Yeah. I was an outsider. Plains Cree in a home full of non-native kids. I was gay and I knew it from an early age. I was different and I felt alone most of the time. I get enough emails from kids who are in the same boat to know that they need my stories as much as I did. Not just native kids but all kinds of kids because adolescence sucks for everybody. I think I help them get through all the bullshit. I try to at least."

He lifted the glass from the table and I noticed the tremor again. It was less obvious but he took a drink and quickly put it down, shoving that hand out of my sight almost as an automatic gesture. That hadn't been there three years ago and I thought it was important but everything about his demeanor said he didn't want me to ask about it and I wasn't going to ruin this moment with him.

"Damn, that must be the best feeling. To create something that makes a difference."

"Yeah. It is.

I reached out to touch him, petting along the skin of his arm and then tangling our fingers together for a second. The contact was electric and his eyes sparked with awareness and something darkly wicked. Flashes of Gareth covering me with his body, forceful and tender and addictive, put my dick on high alert. Muscles tense and desire spiking in the confines of our cocoon of a booth.

I could make a suggestion for the two of us to head to my hotel room and have a phenomenal repeat but I wanted to stretch this time out more. The two of us talking, filling in the blanks of what felt like our unfinished story.

"So, what is the last awesome comic you read?"

His expression registered a split second of confusion at my change of subject but another flash of that elusive grin and he was on board.

"*The Less Than Epic Adventures of TJ and Amal.* I've been re-reading it over and over for a couple of weeks."

I searched the card catalog in my brain, trying to place it because it sounded familiar. I motioned for him to continue. "Keep talking. I know I've read it."

He shifted in the leather seat, excitement about this story radiating through every movement. "Oh man. It's a road trip story with a Bollywood Nerd and a blonde dude with dread-locks. The one guy breaks off his arranged marriage and comes out as gay . . ."

"I know this one. The guy hitches a ride across the country for a graduation." I nudge him with my elbow. "The sex is hot."

"Fuck yeah it is." He eased down in the seat, looking up at me from his semi-recline pose. "The art is so detailed and the story is crazy good. I read it on the web first and then I bought a paper copy from Iron Circus."

"Spike Trotman's company? She's great. I didn't know she had print copies, I'll have to grab one."

"You should."

I had a whisper of a thought that I could talk to Gareth about anything. He was funny and loose when he let his shield down and I found myself responding. I was usually all about work, about closing the deal, and proving my father and all the critics wrong. My plans and ambition didn't allow much room for other people or time to kick back and discuss what was giving us joy at the moment.

This, right here, felt a lot like stretching a muscle that had been neglected and even though I knew I'd be sore tomorrow, I was content to just kick back and just let it happen.

———

When we stood outside St. Nick's two hours later it was dark and Gareth had to get home to take care of his dog and a date with a bunch of teenagers on Federal Hill the next morning. I had work to do, a proposal to put together and a convention to work so ending this evening was something I had to do but not what I wanted.

The street was busy, Fell's Point had an active nightlife with all of the bars and restaurants in the area. The lights of the Inner Harbor were visible on one side while the Domino Sugar sign was reflected in the water where boats were anchored just off the pier. The entire scene had a vibrant energy and I understood why Gareth lived here, right in the middle of life, color, energy, and people.

"So, thanks for dinner," he said, hands shoved in his pockets as the air between us was edged with awkwardness for the first time in hours. It was the end of the evening, "Should I? Will he?" moment of every date.

So, the question was: should I?

I would.

"It's not over yet." I shuffled closer to him, glad that our similarity in height aligned our eyes and mouths perfectly. He licked his bottom lip when he caught me staring at it and the air practically vibrated with awareness. "Dates usually end with a kiss."

"They do?" He asked, his body shifting closer to mine as he spoke and I wondered if he realized he'd done it.

"They do." I reached out and hooked a finger in a belt loop on his jeans and tugged him close enough for our chests to touch. "I want to kiss you."

One of Gareth's large hands cupped my hip, his warmth seeping through my clothes and heading straight for my dick. I was half-hard with anticipation and half-crazed with doubt about how this was going to go. I sent up a quick prayer and locked eyes with him as I eased my mouth closer to his.

"Are you asking for permission?" We were so close now I felt the puff of his breath on my lips and the spark of lust in his eyes as they flickered down to focus on my mouth was all the invitation I needed.

The brush of our mouths together was tentative at first, a test to see if either of us would spook and run. The tease of his taste and the warmth of his body so close but not quite pressed to mine was too much to sustain. I was greedy and I was used to getting what I wanted so I went for it.

I let go of his belt loop and lifted both hands, tracing along his jaw on each side of his face and then tangled my fingers in the sleek silk of his hair. He groaned softly and I crushed my mouth to his, pressing my tongue into the wet warmth of his mouth. Gareth's tongue stroked my own as his hand shifted from my hip to my back, a firm press bringing our groins together in a caress of denim and hard dicks.

He tasted so good. Sweet and dark and something else that made my brain short circuit. It was as good as I remembered. Better. It was déjà vu and it was homecoming. It was something that I hadn't really known I'd missed until now.

A raucous "get a room" interrupted our make-out session and Gareth pulled back, untangling himself from me and I felt the loss of him in my gut. His cheeks were flushed again and his mouth was wet and little swollen but his eyes were sharp and focused on me. I could see the debate of whether he should invite me to his place going on in his mind but that wasn't what I wanted tonight.

Yeah I wanted to strip him down and fuck him but we'd had the one night stand, but we'd never had this. Nothing as simple as a date and kiss good night.

And the night hadn't been anything like what I'd planned when I'd followed him but it was perfect. Exactly the way it should be.

So, to my surprise I heard someone who sounded just like me saying, "Goodnight Gareth."

He paused and I wondered if he would argue with me but he didn't. He nodded and said, "Goodnight" before turning and walking away from me and into the crowd and the night.

I watched him go until I couldn't see him anymore and only when a guy gave me a strange look did I realize I was smiling like a sappy loon. I could feel the panic and stress of what I needed to do, what I had wagered to do, pressing upward but I tamped it down. I was going to take this moment, this feeling and savor it a little while longer.

Tomorrow would be the day to convince Gareth to sign with me.

Not tonight.

Gareth

"Yo, Mr. G. That guy is checking you out."

Proudstar growled low and menacing for a dog with only one eye and a limp. He was a great early warning system but I wasn't sure he'd be able to carry his weight if this situation proved to be a problem.

I placed my sketch pad on the ground and stood, my body tense and ready for a fight if that's what was required. I was a big guy, in a good shape and I'd throw down if somebody tried to mess with these kids. I swiveled in the direction Jamal motioned and stared at Oliver. He was sitting on a nearby bench, holding a carrier with two cups of coffee, posture loose and confident as if he owned the whole damn world.

I envied his swagger. It was the beacon that drew me into his orbit. Over and over.

Fuck, he was pretty. His lean, athletic body was just like his Irish-American dad but the exotic echo of his mother's Korean heritage made for one sexy-as-sin man. Toss in his dark-rimmed glasses, skinny jeans, Converse hightops, and a hoodie and he was the epitome of the New Age nerd who was slowly taking over the world because they refused to follow the rules.

But, what the hell was he doing here?

"Oliver, your stalking is disturbing."

He laughed, the mild irritation in my voice rolling off him like rain on newly-waxed car. It didn't even leave a trace.

"You told me this is where you were going to be this morning. I figured anybody who got up this early on a Saturday morning to draw would need some coffee."

"Mr. G is that your boyfriend? Alison asked me, her bright blue eyes huge in her face with the excitement of possibly witnessing a romantic moment. At sixteen she was all about falling in love and she'd made it her mission to be concerned about the fact that I wasn't dating. It also explained the general theme of her art these days. Lots of embracing couples and hearts. I hoped it passed soon.

"No. He's not my boyfriend," I answered her, weaving my way through the kids scattered across the grass area with Proudstar right on my heels.

"I *am* the guy he went on a date with last night."

I heard the collective "oooh" from the teenagers and felt the laser-focus of their attention on this gay drama like a physical slap. This would come back to haunt me later because teenagers and dirt on their teacher's personal lives were like junkyard dogs with a bone. I made a note to throttle Oliver later for doing this to me.

When I reached him, Oliver rose from the bench with the grace of a dancer, balancing the tray of drinks in one hand, not even a flicker of concern of spilling them on his handsome face.

"Oliver, this is nuts."

"No, this is coffee." He shoved the tray at me and I had no choice but to take it.

Once his hands were free he dropped down into a crouch and held them out for Proudstar to inspect. With the wariness of any shelter dog, he scooted partially behind my legs, his good eye checking out Oliver and then looking up at me for permission.

"It's okay," I assured him and he took a few tentative sniffs of the newcomer before allowing him to scratch him behind the ears.

"What's his name?" Oliver asked.

"Proudstar," I answered, nodding when Oliver looked up at me with curious approval in his expression.

"As in Jon Proudstar? Writer of Tribal Force?"

"One and the same. My first indigenous comic. I loved it."

"I approve of your choice. It suits you," Oliver said with a final pat for my dog. When he rose to his full height, he took one of coffees, his fingers lingering over mine a little too long for it be coincidental. His smirk and then pointed licking of his lips assured me that he knew exactly what he was doing and felt the shudder that wracked my body at the contact. I'd tossed and turned for hours last night, tasting him and reliving the press of his body against mine, the tug of his fingers in my hair.

"Oliver, knock it off. My class is watching our every move and all of it will be on snapchat an hour from now."

He glanced over my shoulder at the sea of teenagers and frowned.

"I didn't count on the mob of underage chaperones," he countered while giving us the requested distance. "Introduce me?"

That. I groaned with resignation and turned towards my class. There was no way I was going to get out of this one.

"Class, this is Oliver Burns. He's the co-owner of Epic Publishing, an independent comic book and graphic novel publisher." I hesitated, wondering if I needed to add more, finally deciding on part of the truth. "We've known each other for a few years and he's here for the convention." I pointed to each kid as I recited their names. "Alison, Jamal, Aaron, Sean,

Joaquin and Stephanie. This is my senior graphic novel seminar at the Baltimore School for the Arts. We meet in different places around the city every other Saturday to transform Baltimore into a story board."

As if on cue, they all lifted their sketchbooks for Oliver to view their work. I admired their confidence. I didn't like anyone looking at my stuff when I was their age. Hell, until yesterday, I'd been hiding behind an online identity. They were so far beyond me, it wasn't even funny.

Oliver handed off his coffee to me and then proceeded to admire the work of each young artist, offering compliments, asking questions, and advice when asked. The kids were eating it up, no doubt thrilled to have the opportunity to rub elbows with a real-life publisher of the industry many of them aspired to join.

I watched him, the last remnants of my lingering irritation from him fucking and running three years ago melting away with each smile my kids flashed in my direction when Oliver said something particularly kind. It was unnerving how easily he enraptured them, how quickly they fell for his particular brand of star power. I knew the power of his looks, his smile, his focused attention. I was still trying to break loose from his tender traps. Or was I?

"Did you know that Mr. G was *the* G?" Jamal asked Oliver, his narrow eye glare turned on me and letting me know once again that he thought my keeping that secret from them was shitty. The first fifteen minutes of our class had been me letting them vent their displeasure at my obvious betrayal.

Oliver shook his head and mimicked Jamal's expression so perfectly they looked like twins. "No. I didn't'."

"That's just so wrong," Jamal griped, shaking his head at me once again.

I was nipping this line of conversation in the bud. There was no way I was being tag-team interrogated by these two. I walked over and handed Oliver his coffee, shaking my head in a way meant to convey, "don't encourage them."

"Look, I did what I did because it was the right thing to do for me. If it makes you feel better, only three people on the entire planet knew I was G: my dad, my agent and his brother."

"But you're famous!" Alison wailed, her face scrunched up with utter horror. "You could have gone to Hollywood. New York!"

"You could have met Anderson Cooper!" Stephanie added with a clap.

"Adam Lambert!" Alison again.

"Ricky Martin," Jamal chimed in, "I mean he's kind of old but he's still totally hot."

I was so over this conversation.

"Oh my God, you have to stop worrying about who I'm dating. Seriously, it's not even appropriate for us to talk about it. Aren't you people supposed to think that I don't even have a life when you're not around?"

"You're only a few years older than we are, Mr. G. You're like a real person. Not like parents or the principal," Stephanie spat out the last bit in a tone that assured me that she thought anyone over forty had one foot in the grave.

At a loss at how to end this insanity, I looked to Oliver for help but he was too busy biting back his laughter to help me out.

"Anderson Cooper *is* really hot," he said, and I shoved him out of the way, gratefully spotting Jamal's mom headed down the path to us. Rescue was in sight and I'd take it no matter what form it arrived in.

The next few moments were spent making sure each kid left with a parent and then packing up my stuff. Oliver helped, holding Proudstar's leash as I loaded the last of everything in my messenger bag and threw away the random bits of trash.

"Where are we headed?" Oliver asked and I chuckled.

"I'm going down to catch the ferry and take it back to Fell's Point and my loft. I'm going camping tonight and have a few things left to do before I can go."

"Camping? Why? That's what Motel 6 is for." Oliver mock shuddered and lobbed his coffee cup into the receptacle before pulling a small manila folder out of his back pocket. "I'll walk with you to the ferry, I need to talk to you."

I cut him a warning glance as I made my way down the path to the ferry landing. "Oliver, I told you I didn't want to talk about signing with Epic. I'm not right for you. You agreed."

"I agreed to table the hard sell for our date last night. I never promised to give up altogether." He reached out and snagged my arm, stopping me in my tracks. "I might not be a Gareth Rain expert but give me some credit for knowing you a little better than Dave from Allied."

"Oliver," I started to pull away but he held me tight, leaning in close and giving me a sexy grin that guaranteed he'd deliver on this promise and so much more if I wanted it.

"Gareth, I know you don't like all the social bullshit: the signings, the meet-n-greets, release tours. I could talk to you until I was blue in the face about how that's all necessary and we need to you do it but I'm not going to waste my time. You're the textbook introvert and the tremor you've been trying to hide is part of it, I'm sure." I gasped and he cocked his head, a soft laugh bubbling up from his chest. "Yeah I noticed and I don't need you to tell me about it right now but I'm hoping you will someday. It doesn't matter because I spent my time putting together a proposal which will get you the maximum exposure and distribution without all of that stuff. Both of those things mean more money in your pocket. It's not easy and not the norm but it can be done. Epic can do it."

Oliver let go of me, sliding the envelope into the front

pocket of my messenger bag with a final pat. He turned, walking down the path towards the ferry, his long stride forcing me to jog a bit to catch up.

"You should give the proposal to Neal," I said.

"Already emailed it to him this morning. That's your copy."

"We have another offer from Tradehouse."

"I welcome the competition."

"You're pushy," I grumbled, passing him on the downhill and reaching the ferry before he did. I paid the fare, leading Proudstar onto the boat as Oliver got his ticket right behind me. We settled onto seats, watching silently as a mother and four rowdy boys joined us, their shoving and shouting causing her to look at us in silent apology.

Oliver waved her off with a smile before he turned to me, the smile gone and replaced by an earnestness I hadn't seen on him before. Oliver was charming and slick and aggressive but this expression had none of that and it made me wonder if this was a side of him he didn't let people see very often. I'd had glimpses of a big heart and quiet strength and deep cuts that night we'd spent together but they'd vanished with him the next morning.

"Gareth. No angles. No gimmicks. No hidden clauses. We can offer you distro and marketing support with creative ways for you to add what the fans need socially: videos, live chats. Minimal face-face interaction. Read it and think about it. I think we could be amazing together." He considered his words for a moment and a trace of his old grin came back with the lightest brushes of his fingers on my arm. "Well, you know, amazing outside of the bedroom."

I rolled my eyes and leaned back against the side of the boat. "I'll read it."

"Awesome." He said, sounding like he'd already won some contest.

"I just said I'd read it."

"I just know that if you read it then you'll sign with Epic,"

"How do you walk having to carry all that ego around?" I asked, standing as the ferry pulled up the Fell's Point pier.

Oliver was close on my heels, leaning down to pet Proud-star on his head. The boys jumped out of their seats, racing for the gangway and jostling the two of us in their battle to be first. The mom followed, yelling that this wasn't their stop. One of the boys climbed on the railing to try to beat his sibling and all of us saw the moment when he lost his grip and started to fall. Oliver rushed forward to grab the kid and tripped and the last part I saw of him was the bottom of his sneakers as he fell overboard and into the water with a loud, wet splash.

Oliver

"Your clothes are in the dryer. Are you warm enough in that robe?"

"Yeah, the shower helped. That water was fucking cold. And gross." I yelled across his loft, not wanting to stop my nosy perusal of all the photographs he had hanging on the wall and sitting on the bookshelves. I pulled the flannel closer around me and inhaled the scent of Gareth and his particular brand of soap and detergent. "These photos are amazing."

I felt him come up behind me before I heard him, silent on his bare feet in defiance of his sheer bulk and size.

"Adam Woodson, Neal's brother took most of them. He's fucking fantastic," he said before opening a cabinet to reveal a turntable. I watched him crouch down and pull a plastic-sleeve wrapped vinyl record album from it, gently removing the disc and placing it with gentle reverence on the turntable. A quick placement of the needle, a couple of scratches, and the Motown sounds of R&B filled the loft.

"Who's this?" I asked, unable to pinpoint the name even though the voice was crazy familiar.

"Smokey Robinson. He's my favorite," Gareth answered,

putting away the album cover and closing the cabinet. "He's playing at the MGM Grand at National Harbor next month but I couldn't get tickets. They sold out too fast."

"You love Motown?" I inquired, turning my gaze back to the photographs.

There were a variety of images. Some in color but most of them were in black and white. Long range shots of a village nestled between large, hulking mountains under miles of blue sky. Some of them bore the sign of "Rocky Boy Indian Reservation" – the place where Gareth had grown up for the first part of his life. The majority of the pictures were of people, young and old, all bearing a resemblance to Gareth, especially a man who shyly smiled up from a rocking chair on a porch sitting next to Gareth. I guessed that he was his father.

Gareth eased up next to me and looked over my shoulder, his bulk pressed up against my side. I leaned back into him enjoying the moment and the closeness and this strange thing that was happening between us. It was like the last three years hadn't happened and I hadn't left. I'd stayed and we'd spent the rest of the convention together and after . . . well, that was happening now.

"I love Motown. My dad listened to it all the time." He pointed at the rocking chair photo I'd noticed a few moments earlier. "I knew that when the music was playing, then it was going to be a good night at home."

I turned to face him, hoping he wouldn't bristle and run at my questions. "Did he drink?"

"Oh yeah. Such a cliché, right?" Gareth's gaze focused on the picture behind me and I could see all those years of pain and fear he'd experienced as a child play across his face and cloud the usual spark in his dark eyes. "He broke my arm one night and that's when I was placed at the orphanage. I was ten years old and I was really angry with him for a long time."

"What changed? What happened to make you forgive him?"

I had my own issues with my father and I couldn't imagine what it would take for us to get to the point where we could sit anywhere and smile. I just didn't see it ever happening.

"He had to go to the hospital for a fall he'd taken down some stairs and while he was there they helped him stop drinking." Gareth looked at me then and my breath caught at the pain, regret, sympathy and fear I saw there now. Whatever he was about to tell me, I knew in my gut it didn't end with his father. Gareth was going to have to carry that burden as well. I reached and took his hand in mine, lacing our fingers together in an act of support and comfort. "When he finally got sober they noticed the essential tremor and figured out that he'd been self-medicating with the booze his entire life. He didn't drink because he was irresponsible, he started drinking because of his condition. I didn't wipe it all away but it made his behavior forgivable. It gave us a place to start over. I spend several months out there with him every year. It's not what it would have been if he'd never started drinking but it's good."

"And this tremor . . ."

"I have it too. It's hereditary," he answered, his voice barely above a whisper. "Medication controls it now but it's in my hands and while I'm exploring every kind of adaptive drawing tools and resources, I might not be able to draw one day."

And that was why he was looking for a distro deal. To maximize his earnings for the time when he wouldn't be able to produce more content. Gareth really couldn't afford to take a bad deal.

And the thought that this talented man might not be able to tell his stories and make the worlds swirling in his mind come to life on the page made my chest hurt. I lifted his hand to my mouth and kissed every finger, pouring every bit of what I was feeling into every press of my lips.

49

"Don't pity me," he said, his voice rough with emotion and edged with anger. "I don't want that."

"It's not pity but I am sad and angry and frustrated that your talent is being threatened by this thing. The kids need you and the Warriors." I struggled to find the words to describe what I was feeling but all I could muster was a growl and "this sucks."

Gareth squeezed my hand and pulled me to the center of the large open room, wrapping an arm around my waist and pulling me close.

"Dance with me," he asked, his expression bright with mischief. He wanted to move off the dire and have some fun. I could do that.

"I didn't think you danced." I said as we moved slowly to the sensual, sexy beat of the music.

"I never said that I didn't dance. I just don't like to dance in public. I'm not very good."

"Well, I'm not any good either." I looped an arm tighter around his waist and pulled him even closer, so close we were moving as one body. Reading each other's signals, cues. No one leading and no one following. We were just together. "It's just a great excuse to hold someone close."

"You never need an excuse for that."

"No?"

"Never," he said, leaning down to press our cheeks together, stubble on stubble making me shiver with desire. I loved scruff on a man, it heightened every kiss, every brush of the skin. My cock got hard underneath the thin layer of the robe and I knew he could feel it but we didn't move to that level – not yet. We swayed together as one song slid into another, letting the moments spool out into something neither of us could have predicted and I couldn't have orchestrated.

Lost in the sensation of the warmth, strength and spicy scent of Gareth, I almost didn't hear him when he spoke.

"Why did you leave that night?"

He didn't have to specify which night. There was only one of import between us. The one that felt unfinished and raw.

"I had to. I wanted to stay."

Gareth shifted back, separating us only enough to look me in the eye. "And wanting to stay was a problem."

"Yeah." I sighed, leaning my forehead against his shoulder, parsing through the right words to describe the devil that drove me. "I had to leave because I had to keep moving. Ellis and I were just starting Epic and everybody knew my dad hadn't backed my decision to not follow him into real estate. He'd talked about it widely, person-to-person and in the media. Mogul Michael Burns thought his son would fail. Hell, he wants me to fail so he'll be right."

Gareth tipped my chin up with a finger, his eye crinkled with humor and filled with understanding. "So, you're telling me that you let me wake up alone in that bed because you have daddy issues?"

I barked out a laugh at his accurate and humorous summary. I pressed a quick kiss to his mouth before continuing. "Yes. I'm a garden variety head case. One of the sons driven to succeed by the constant criticism and lack of support of their overbearing and likely insecure fathers. At least that's what my therapist tells me." I sighed again and answered his question. "I left that morning because I wanted to stay. I wanted another night and another morning. I didn't have time for forever. Hell, I didn't have time for a short-term relationship."

I didn't have the time now but that wasn't getting my ass out of the door. What was I doing here? Why wasn't I doing the hard sell to get him to sign those papers in his bag and then hitting the door? Gareth was 200 pounds of sexy, muscled trouble for me, plain and simple.

"Look, Oliver, I've kept up with you and Ellis in the media. I know your reputation of being a shark, a guy who is always working the angles and trying eliminate the competition. I'm not trying to get in the way of your success, just don't work angles on me."

I thought about the bet. About why I'd sought him out and followed him to the bar last night. Once there, my reasons had shifted. And while they weren't completely different, business and pleasure were getting mixed up and the lines were blurry.

I knew I wanted to pursue this thing with Gareth. It might peter out in two weeks or I might find myself in this loft a year from now. I didn't know much except that I didn't want to leave right now.

I traced the curve of his jaw lightly before sliding my fingers into the silk of his hair, cupping his head and drawing him closer to me. He moaned and the vibration of it on my lips went straight to my cock. And when he nuzzled in close and licked across my bottom lip, I knew I wasn't going anywhere.

Gareth was impatient and he covered my mouth with his own and pushed his tongue inside. This was the dominant, take-charge Gareth from that night and the combination of him and the flashes of what I knew he could do with his hands, lip and cock made me instantly dizzy with desire. I wouldn't be dumb enough to sneak out again.

"Where's your bedroom?" I asked, dragging my hands down his back, finding the hem of his shirt and tugging it off and throwing it on the floor.

"You're always so impatient," he murmured against the curve of my neck before nipping my earlobe. "I'm not going anywhere. We've got all the time in the world."

I opened the belt on the robe and let I fall open, grabbing his hand and leading it down to my rock hard cock. He needed to feel just how impatient I was. Just how much I wanted him. Gareth gasped and then groaned as I fucked his grip, urging him to stroke me tight and fast.

I wasn't idle, unbuckling his belt and unbuttoning his jeans while he worked my cock. My hands were shaking but I managed to get his zipper down without injuring him and found him gloriously naked underneath the denim. I locked eyes with him and raised my hand, making a big show of licking my palm before I wrapped my fingers around his dick and started stroking.

"Fuck, that's so hot," Gareth murmured before taking my mouth again in a bruising kiss. His enthusiastic need almost threw us both off balance but I widened my stance and kept us both from toppling to the floor. Gareth planted both of his hands on my ass, kneading the muscles there before pulling my cheeks apart and swiping the softest of touches against my hole.

"God, yes." I stroked him, squeezing gently around the head on every pass to encourage him to shove it inside my tight heat. I wanted that. So fucking much. I whimpered, torn between needing him to stroke me harder or to massage my hole. He just teased, keeping me on edge and under his control.

I loved it.

"I want you, Oliver."

That was all I needed to hear and stepped back from him, letting the robe slip from my body onto the floor. I fully intended to order him to point us towards a bed but the sight of his long, tight body, bronze skin exposed in the afternoon light filtering in through the windows made my mouth water. His cock, hard and thick, jutted out from a nest of black curls and I dropped to my knees in front of him.

I grabbed his jeans and shoved them all the way down, leaving them in a puddle at his feet before I grabbed his dick and swallowed him whole. He was big, his smoky flavor filling my mouth. Gareth reached back and gripped the edge of his leather sofa for balance on a groan that rumbled up from his belly.

"You're so fucking good at that," he gasped out, gripping the back of my head to hold me in place. I looked up and our eyes locked as he slowly began to fuck my face, shoving his huge meat a little bit farther in with each thrust. I relaxed, wanting to take him as far as he could go, loving the way he looked at me every time he sunk into my wet heat.

I sucked him off for several minutes, stoking my own hard cock as our desire ratcheted higher and hotter with each moan and thrust. I needed him inside me and I let out a sigh of relief when he pulled out and lifted me to my feet.

"God, I want you. Let me fuck you, baby."

There was only one answer.

"Yes."

Gareth

All I wanted to do was get inside Oliver and fuck him until he'd never want to leave my bed.

It was foolish, Neanderthal. The man had just admitted that his work came first, he had no time for anything but a fuck buddy and I was spinning tales of dates and nights sleeping beside him, and mornings of lazy sex in covers warmed all night by our bodies. I wasn't going to get it but I could have this. I could have right now and I was going to take it.

"Follow me," I took his hand and led him over to an alcove tucked away on the side of the loft. Japanese shoji slid back and forth on a track and shielded the bedroom from the rest of the space. I slid one back and we both were reflected in the large, framed mirror leaning against the wall next to the bed.

We looked good together. My dark skin against his paler tones, our similar heights but my bulk contrasted with his finely muscled and toned limbs. I couldn't wait to see how we looked when we were fucking, bodies slick with sweat and flushed with arousal.

Oliver let go of my hand and climbed on the bed. I followed, huffing out a bark of surprise when he pushed me down onto my back and climbed on top, straddling my thighs. He leaned over me, his long hard dick pressed between us as he teased my lips with a hint of a kiss.

I chuckled, amused that he thought that was how this was going to go. I gripped his hips and tumbled us both over, ending up with Oliver beneath me on his back. He laughed, looping his arms around my neck and his legs around my waist. Our cocks rubbed together, the perfect kind of friction as we kissed, tongues tangling, hot and wet as our bellies grew slick with our precome.

This felt so good. Amazing. But it wasn't enough.

I pulled back, sitting between his spread thighs. I pushed his thighs father apart, loving the view of his hard dick, tight balls and tight hole. I lightly traced a path down his shaft and between his cheeks, stroking the pucker and watching him writhe beneath me.

"Are you going to let me fuck you, Oliver? I want to bury my dick so deep inside you. Can I?"

He let out a long groan as I pressed against his opening, teasing just how good I was going to feel inside him.

"Yes, fuck me. Please, Gareth. Please."

I leaned over the side of the bed, opening the drawer to my nightstand and pulled out condoms and lube. I threw them down of the bed, ignoring his look of confusion as I eased down between his legs and licked his shaft from bottom to top before sucking him down in one pass.

Oliver squirmed beneath me, his hips bucking upward to fuck deep into my mouth. His fingers were tangled in my hair, something I knew he loved, and the sting of his tugs as he held my head in place only made it feel that much better.

"Gareth, please...." he moaned and shoved me away from him. "I'm so close but I want to come with you inside me."

I leaned over his body, taking the kiss he offered and

grinding my dick against his thigh. I sat up and grabbed the lube, tossing it to him.

"Get yourself ready. I want to watch."

Oliver sat up, shoving me down onto my back as he straddled me once again. I watched as he poured lube over his fingers, arched his back and pressed a finger inside his hole. I groaned, my fingers digging into the flesh of his thighs as he rocked on his finger, loosening his body for me. I could see it all in the mirror: his finger sliding in and out of body and his hard cock leaking fluid all over my belly. When he withdrew his finger and put more lube on several digits, I coated my own and reached around when he inserted two of his fingers in his channel.

"Can you take more?" I asked, waiting for the nod of his head to give me the greenlight.

I slid my finger inside his tight heat alongside his own, catching his mouth in a kiss when he fell forward on hiss and a "yes, fuck".

"Does that feel good?" I asked, looking over his sweat-slicked shoulder to watch the show in the mirror behind us.

"I need your cock, baby. Please."

His whispered plea and the combination of our reflection amped it up about two-hundred percent and I knew I needed to get inside him now or it was all going to be over before it began.

I grabbed a condom and suited up, adding extra slick to the rubber. Oliver lined me up with his hole and lowered himself down my length. He stopped frequently to get used to my invasion, the burn also flushing his cheeks. He was tight and hot and I wanted to move but I waited him out, breathing out a sigh of relief when he finally moved against me, giving me the friction I craved.

"Oh, fuck," I moaned. It wasn't pretty or articulate but it was the best I could do as Oliver began to ride me up and down at a steady pace. His hands traveled all over my chest, tweaking my nipples and pressing ravenous, open-mouthed kisses on my skin. I felt like he was devouring me and I let him. It had been too long since the last time I'd had this with him and I was soaking it all in.

When he leaned over and murmured against my mouth, "more" I took the cue and flipped us both over. I hooked his knees over my arms and drove inside him, hard and fast, rolling my hips to find the spot that made him crazy.

"Oh, yes. Harder. Please, baby." His mantra was low and guttural, hitching a breath every time I stroked over his prostate.

He lifted his arms over his head, his long body stretched out under me in complete surrender. I could take him any way I wanted. I could do to him anything I wanted. He was mine. When I reached down and wrapped my fingers around his cock, stroking him in rhythm with my thrusts he went wild under me. Eyes shut, fingers gripping the sheets bunched above his head, the only sounds in the room were our moans and the slap of our bodies together.

"Oliver, look at me." I demanded and I waited to the couple of seconds it took for him to obey. His pupils were blown, his lips swollen with the imprint of his teeth marks, his body slick with sweat and precome and lube. "You're so fucking hot. You love being fucked don't you?"

He nodded, one hand lowering to stroke his cock but I batted it away.

"I think you need to see yourself. I want you to watch me fuck you."

I carefully pulled out, urging him over onto all fours in front of the mirror. He was slow at first, a little sex-drunk but once he caught a glimpse of us in the mirror he was all in. He looked over his shoulder at me, wiggled his ass and gave me a sexy grin that made my dick pulse.

"Move forward, closer to the mirror."

He followed my lead, his whole body wracked by a shiver when I placed his palms on the mirror. All of Oliver was exposed this way and I watched as he took in every detail, waiting for him to meet my eyes in the reflection.

"Come on Gareth. Do it."

I moved in close behind him and slowly thrust inside. This new position was tighter and the combination of his grip on me and the visual told me that I wasn't going to last long. I took it slow, trying to draw it out, trying to keep this feeling going but it wasn't possible.

I couldn't tear my eyes away from us. We were perfect. Filthy and debauched but perfect together. I let my hands roam all over his chest, across his thighs finally taking his cock in hand and beginning a steady stroke. Oliver pushed back against the thrust of my dick, effectively fucking himself on every movement.

I knew he was close. A flush of heat spread across his chest and his moans grew louder, echoing off the high ceilings and exposed beams of my loft. I loved it, soaked in every sound, every cry.

"Get yourself off on me, baby. Use me to feel good," I said, urging him on as his movement became more erratic and frantic. I anchored my one free hand on his hips and increased the speed of my thrusts, feeling the exact moment his body stiffened with his orgasm.

I watched him shudder and writhe as his cum splattered the mirror. I leaned over him, covering his back and wrapping my arms around him as he came down from the high, nuzzling our cheeks together when he leaned back for a deep, slow kiss.

He pushed back against me and I sped up my pace, crying out against his shoulder when I felt the wave of pleasure roll over me. I thrust through it, emptying myself inside the condom until all I wanted to do was collapse.

I eased out of his body, stripping off the rubber and tossing it in the waste bin. I pulled Oliver back against me and we sank down into the tangle of sweat-damp sheets. I couldn't move. He didn't move. We both breathed heavily as we reluctantly returned to earth.

The shadows were moving across the room. It was late afternoon and outside my loft I could hear the sounds of the restaurants getting ready for the dinner crowd and early commuters heading home from work.

"If I ask you to stay, will you be here in the morning?" I asked, biting his shoulder when he took too long to answer.

"Ouch," he said, rolling over to face me. "That better not leave a mark."

"I already left my mark on you Oliver, don't you know that?" It was out before I could stop it and I held my breath to see how he'd react. It wasn't a declaration or anything but it was an outright acknowledgement that this wasn't just one night three years ago and it wasn't just this moment. It could be more. It was more.

"That's what scares me," he said, finally breaking the silence that had stretched a little too long.

"If I tell you that it scares me too, will you be here in the morning?"

He pondered for another long moment and I'd begun to believe that this was the last time, part two. But then he surprised me.

Leaning forward to press a kiss against my mouth, he looked me in eyes when he answered, "I'll be here in the morning."

Gareth

Oliver was there in the morning.

I'd woken this morning with his body wrapped around mine, his fingers tangled in my hair. I'd watched him sleep for a while until I started to feel like a creepy stalker and then I'd carefully left the bed just long enough to grab my sketchbook and memorialize him onto a few pages to use as a reference for later. I had a feeling that there might be a new character added to the GHOST WARRIORS universe if I could figure out what to do with a sexy, fast-talking man with a wicked spark in his eyes.

When Oliver had woken, I'd quickly changed that character to a flesh-eating zombie troll who murdered anyone who dared to wake him from his nap underneath the bridge.

Oliver Burns was not a morning person.

I was used to people who couldn't handle human interaction before having a cup of coffee but Oliver needed time, not caffeine, to make him fit for public consumption. Lots of time.

It took that time, a shower and a change of clean clothes to transform Oliver into anything remotely resembling a Prince – I guessed the charming part only happened after noon.

So, his need for clothing and a morning meeting for him was what found me in the elevator of the Renaissance Hotel at in the Inner Harbor with two coffees, a bran muffin, cinnamon bun and two bananas and headed back up to Oliver's room.

The hallway was empty as I made my way back to his suite but as I came to the door I heard voices inside. One was definitely Oliver and the other was a woman. I looked at my watch. If she was his morning meeting, she was an hour early. I just hoped Oliver's mood had improved or he wasn't going to be sealing a deal or anything else today.

The bar was engaged so the door stood ajar and I slipped quietly inside. I wanted to get a better idea of who was here before I barged in and interrupted something important. If he needed a few minutes I could read over his proposal again before I met with Neal later today.

The deal was sweet. Oliver had fashioned a scenario where I could produce new content and market it with only nominal face-to-face interactions with fans. I'd use live digital events, virtual signings and structured meet-n-greets when absolutely necessary. This way I wouldn't have to worry as much about people noticing my tremors if they did occur. Epic would provide full-scale distribution and logistics support and I would retain creative control over my new content and total control over the webcomic. This was not a typical deal for Epic. It was special just for me and it might be the right deal.

A deal I could trust with a man I could trust.

Thanks to Oliver.

The sound of my name from the other room caught my attention and I stopped to listen, moving closer to the doorway. I hated to eavesdrop but I was just too curious about what they had to say about me.

"Oliver, have you closed the deal with Gareth? We've only got a couple more days here and I thought you said you'd have it wrapped by now."

"Ellis, I gave him the proposal and he's going to talk about it with Neal today. It's a great deal, a tailor-made deal. I'll sign him, don't worry about it."

"I'm not worried, it's your money," his partner said, her voice tinged with resignation. I knew that tone. I think you used it a lot when you were around Oliver. He never did what you expected and that could try the patience of a saint. "I still can't believe you made that stupid bet with Dave. That's just a fucking waste of money."

Bet? What the fuck was that about? I shifted even closer, not even a little bit embarrassed about eavesdropping now.

"Ellis, I told you that I'm not going to lose so don't worry about it." He chuckled and I could just picture him waving off her concern. Cocky as always. Confident in his ability to get what he wanted. "I'll sign him and I'll win."

My entire body went cold as my brain caught up with what I'd heard. Oliver had made a bet that he could sign me. A bet. A wager that was all about stroking his ego and being the one to win every time. I was nothing but a big conquest to him, another commodity to gain in his quest to prove his father wrong.

I stepped into the living area of the suite, clenching my hands into a fist with my effort not to punch him in the face. Who was I fooling? My hands were shaking, the tremors made worse by the stress of the moment and the extra adrenaline coursing through my body. I cursed my stupid fucking body because I was hurting and all I wanted to do right now was hurt Oliver. Since he clearly didn't give a shit about me, it had to be physical pain because emotions weren't even part of the equation.

Oliver saw me first, his smile widening as he walked towards me. I held up my hands to stop him. If he touched me I couldn't predict what I would do. I just wanted him to tell me the truth just one fucking time and then get the hell out of here.

"So, how much was I worth?" He looked confused, I didn't have time or the patience to wait for him to catch up. "The bet, Oliver. How much was the goddam bet?"

My voice shook, breaking on the last two words and I wanted to howl at the moon in frustration and embarrassment. But my delivery didn't matter because his face fell, his complexion going pale and ashy as he connected the dots between my question and what I'd heard.

"Oh fuck," Ellis said, her voice full of dread as she turned to face me. Her eyes were pleading, begging me not to kill her stupid partner I supposed.

"Gareth, you have to " Oliver said but I had no patience for what he thought I had to do.

"Save it Oliver." I took a deep breath and steadied myself as much as I could. I could feel my avalanche coming but I was determined to get my answers. "I heard you. I know what I heard and all I want to know is how much? How much did you bet Dave? Simple question. Simple answer."

The silence stretched out between us, strained and filled with pain and anger and regret. Oliver was sorry he'd gotten caught. I was sorry I'd been duped while I tried to ignore the shards of glass ramming into my chest. I just needed him to tell me so that I could leave and fall apart in private. I might be a fool but I'd never let him see how much power he had to hurt me.

"Oliver." The warning in my voice made him jump and it loosened his tongue.

"Five thousand dollars," he said, his hands reaching out to me but I took a step back. Away from him and away from all the pain he brought with him.

"Wow," I whistled long and low. "I had no idea I was so valuable.

"Gareth, it's not what you think. It has nothing to do with us."

I held up my hand, stopping what would surely be another lie, another angle. This was exactly what I thought it was.

And it was also over.

"You did me a huge favor sneaking out on me three years ago and I just realized how lucky I was. You treat everything and everyone as a commodity, another tool to help you prove daddy wrong and stroke your ego. But this isn't a game to me Oliver. This is my life, my gift, my heart and I'm done with you." I turned to leave but I had one more thing I needed to say. "You know, your father is wrong about you. You have *exactly* what it takes to make it. He should be proud."

Oliver

Every part of my body was screaming to follow Gareth but I couldn't move.

I couldn't catch my breath. My entire body was cold, ice rushing through my veins, under my skin and a huge block of it was sitting in my belly. But I couldn't stay here and do nothing. Doing nothing would only result in my losing Gareth.

And I'd just found him again.

I started moving towards the door but Ellis pulled me back.

"Oliver, what are you going to do?"

"I'm going to explain to him. I'm going to calm him down and make him see that he's got this all wrong."

I tried to wrench my arm out of her grasp but she dug in and held me in place. "Oliver, what does he have wrong?"

Her question was like a slap across my face. It wasn't just the words, it was the way she said them. And the way she was looking at me. Like she was disappointed. Like she was ashamed. Like I'd gone too far and she was done with me.

"What does he have wrong, Oliver?" She asked again as she let go of me and sunk down on the couch. Ellis ran her fingers through her hair in frustration as she parsed through whatever she needed to say. My gut clenched with dread because I knew I wasn't going to like what she was going to say and I knew that it was probably because it was the truth. "Oliver I've known you for a long time and I love you but sometimes you make it so hard. You're brilliant but you're always corrupting it with your need to sharpen every victory into an arrow to aim at your dad." She looked up at me, her expression full of all the affection I knew she had for me but it was also full of pity. The one thing I did not want from her or anyone else. I was nobody's "poor little rich kid". "I was at that convention three years ago, do you remember? I was with you the first time you saw Gareth. You were thunderstruck. Mute for the first time in your life over some twenty-year old kid with long hair and eyes only for you. I got a front row seat to the connection you two clearly had and I crossed my fingers that you'd let it happen because you'd never let it happen before."

"I loved you Ellis," I rushed in to say, making sure she understood how much she meant to me. I tried to have that with her. I'd really tried but it never happened for us. Because of me. Because I couldn't let myself go that far. Not even with her. "I did. I do."

"I know all that Oliver but we both know it's not the forever kind." Her smile was watery but still determined. "I also know that Gareth Rain probably is that kind. You two had something and by the look on your face I think you still do. That guy is nuts about you because the kind of hurt he's carrying only happens when you care that much."

"And that's why I need to go get him and make him understand," I insisted, pointing towards the door and my only chance to make this right. Every second that passed by was a second he hardened his heart against me. It was another layer of stone I'd have to blast through. "The bet meant nothing. We can still win. He can still sign with Epic and take the money.

He can donate it to that shelter he did the charity signing for the other day and we can be together."

"No, you can't Oliver. You can't have both. Gareth just made that perfectly clear." She stood and moved to stand in front of me, reaching up with one hand to tenderly cup my face. "Your dad is an asshole and he doesn't deserve the amazing son he has. But his failure to realize it is on him but the way you let him warp your entire life, your entire approach to life is all on you. This one is on you because you know better, you knew better but you didn't do the right thing. When you realized you and Gareth had more than just a potential contract between you, you should have told him about the bet."

I knew she was right. This was like one of those stupid plotlines of those movies where you find yourself shouting at the screen because the hero fails to do the one thing that won't fuck up his life. Be honest. Not just with the person he's betraying but with himself.

And I wasn't honest with myself.

I'd lied to myself for so long, relying on my fast talk and charm to get me out of anything remotely complicated. I'd used my ambition as a shield to protect myself from getting hurt but this time it had backfired and the shield had turned into a weapon and hurt someone I deeply cared about. Someone I could probably love. The forever kind of love.

"Your dad wins every time you do something to prove him wrong, Oliver. He wins." Ellis reached up on her tiptoes and pressed a kiss to my cheek before moving towards the door.

"Wait, what do I do?" I could hear the panic in my voice, it was a perfect embodiment of the ice-cold fear gripping my heart. She was right but I didn't know how to break the chain. I didn't know how to fix this. "How do I get him back?"

"It's simple, Oliver. In order to win this time, you're going to have to lose."

Gareth

"You have two offers on the table, Gareth."

I paused the task of making coffee to look over at where Neal sat on my couch. He was casual today, absent was his typical uniform of suit and tie, but his expression was still the same serious one he always wore when he was in lawyer mode. I'd spent the last three days in this loft, trying not to check my phone for messages from Oliver and trying to ignore the crushing weight that sat constantly on my chest.

I needed to get away from here but I couldn't leave. I still had a few more weeks of my seminar to teach and I couldn't leave the kids hanging this late in the semester. I wanted to go home, back to Rocky Boy and my father. It was testament to just how fucked up I was that the solace I sought was in a place where I'd spent the majority of my life hating. But the mountains were a place I could hide. I could hike with Proudstar and never see anyone for days. I'd stay up there until this didn't hurt so much anymore.

"Allied didn't come back with another offer, did they? Because that is a non-starter," I said, grabbing the two mugs of coffee and heading towards the living area. I only spilled a little bit of the liquid, my right hand having a mild tremor this morning but Proudstar rushed over to lick up the puddle.

"No," Neal started and then hesitated, his expression betraying all of his concern for me. He'd been great the last two days. He'd given me space but also arranged for food delivery to make sure that I ate. But he was scheduled to go back to Montana tomorrow and he'd insisted on having this meeting face-to-face. "Gareth, you have an offer from Tradestone and one from Epic."

That was . . . unexpected.

"Well, you can throw that one in the trash. There is no way in hell I'm taking anything from Epic."

"I hear you, but I think you probably need to read this." He held out an envelope to me. "It's still sealed with your name on it." When I took it from him he picked up another from the pile of papers spread out in front of him. "This one was addressed to me. From Oliver."

Now, I was really confused. "What did it say?"

Neal looked down at the paper, reading verbatim. "Epic Publishing hereby withdraws its offer and throws its support behind Tradestone." He looked at me, shrugging his shoulders. "The Tradestone offer is exactly the one that Oliver sent to us. You know how much I liked that one, the terms were fair and it suited your personal needs very well. I'm hoping that the letter in your hands will fill in the gaps."

I was confused. Utterly confused. I wasn't surprised that Oliver withdrew his offer, with how things had gone down, it was the only thing he could do. But to throw his support to Tradestone? To give his ideas to Tradestone? That wasn't like him at all.

It was like he'd gone out of his way to make sure he lost.

I turned the envelope over in my hands, noting his sure, broad handwriting on the outside. I slid my finger under the flap and pulled out a folded sheet of a paper. Two other

72

smaller pieces of paper fell out as well and I turned them over to read what was printed on them. I sucked in a breath in shock. They weren't real. Couldn't be.

"What is it?" Neal asked, his body leaning forward as he strained to read the text.

"Two tickets to see Smokey Robinson at the MGM Grand." I read further. "VIP tickets . I get access to backstage and the meet-n-greet with him."

"That shows been sold out for months. I remember you telling me about it."

"I know." I placed the tickets on the table and opened the other sheet of paper. It was covered in Oliver's handwriting.

Gareth:

I wouldn't blame you if you tore this up without reading it but I hope you don't. I fucked up. I never should have made that bet and I should have told you about it once I realized that we were more than just one night and more than just a publishing deal. And if I'm going for total honesty here, I never should have left you in the hotel room three years ago. I should have stayed and I should have seen what we could have been. I'm sorry that I have been such a coward. I'm sorry that I let my drive to prove my father wrong get between us. I'm sorry. I never wanted to hurt you Gareth. If I could do it all differently I would. We'd have three years of memories behind us and I would be a better man.

I don't want you to miss out on a publishing deal to get you what you need for now and the future. I still think my proposal for you was the best one out there so I took it to Tradestone and told them to use it. Danny Bryce is a good man and it's a good company. He's honest and he'll honor the terms of the deal if you sign with him. Ask Neal what he thinks. He is also a good man and he'll recognize another one when he sees him.

The tickets are for you. I know a guy who knows a guy . . . enjoy the concert.

I'm sorry.
Oliver

I refolded the paper and let his words wash over me. None of it made sense. I looked at Neal who was sitting patiently, waiting for me to tell him what the letter said.

"He gave his proposal to Tradestone." I stuttered out a laugh that fell somewhere between a chuckle and a sob. "He gave them his proposal and told me to sign with them. He said that Danny Bryce was a good man and would honor the deal."

Neal nodded. "He is and he would."

My lips twisted into a wry smile at that. "He said you'd say that too."

I didn't have to voice the question between the lines of my statement. Neal knew what I was asking him. He was not a man who made rash decisions or gave off-the-cuff advice. He was careful, analytical and I valued his friendship and his counsel more than I could say.

"I think I'm a good judge of character." Neal took a sip of coffee, debating internally what he was going to say next. "Oliver screwed up and he's fighting this demon with his father and he was wrong. But he's a good man underneath all of the spin and machinations. He admits when he's wrong and he tries his best to make it right. There are no perfect men out there, only imperfect ones who try to be better every day."

"So, what should I do?"

"I think you should take the deal with Tradestone."

"What should I do about Oliver?" I knew I sounded like a middle school girl but my professional life was the easiest question on the table.

Neal shook his head, placing his mug down on the table. "I don't give relationship advice. I wouldn't even know what to charge for it but I'll tell you this: you need to decide if Oliver is the man for you, imperfections and all. Good men are hard to find but they are worth taking the risk."

Gareth

Tracking Oliver down was easier than I expected it would be.

For all of his bravado and fast-talking, underneath it all he was a sentimental soul who was easy to predict when you knew him. And I think I was finally starting to understand Oliver Burns. Or at least I wanted to understand him.

I opened the huge, wooden double doors of St. Nick's and stepped into the air-conditioned mid-afternoon gloom of the building. I blinked rapidly, trying to force my eyes to adjust and focus as quickly as possible. Now that I was here, I wanted to find him and get this done, get us back on track.

Because I wanted an us.

As fucked up a rollercoaster it was definitely going to be . . . I wanted it. I wanted him.

Moving from the old narthex I shifted into the large open bar area and scanned all of the patrons. It was the middle of the afternoon, so it wasn't full but even if it had been packed on a Saturday during Fleet Week, I would have been able to pinpoint Oliver in the crowd.

The long, sleek line of his body. His almost elegant demeanor even in the middle of bar in Baltimore, Maryland.

He was in our booth, nursing a beer as he contemplated a new plan in the condensation on the glass. He was so lost in own thoughts that he didn't look up when I approached.

"Oliver."

He raised his head and looked at me and the pain and regret and sadness I saw there made me reach out to grasp the edge of the table for support. Oliver looked lost. Shattered.

He looked like I'd broken his heart.

He looked like I felt.

"You're an asshole, you know that?"

His eyes widened in surprise at my words but even in the lowlight of the bar I could see the hint of hope creeping into his eyes.

"I am."

"You lied to me."

"I did."

He stood, moving out from the booth. Oliver shifted closer to me but not close enough. I closed the distance between us but didn't touch him, not yet. If I did that I might not say what I needed to say.

"Then why the fuck should I give you the chance to hurt me again?" I didn't like the way my pain and insecurity coated every one of my words but I didn't do anything to scale it back. This was important, too important to worry about appearances or pride.

Oliver stared at me, the furrow between his eyes deep with his concentration and the effort to say whatever he was going to say. When he spoke, it took two tries to get the words out and even then, they were choked with his own pain and regret.

"Because I think that in the end nobody is going to love you like I'm going to love you if you give me the chance."

"Oliver."

"Gareth, hear me out," he said, gaining momentum and courage with every breath. "I'm not perfect and I'm going to fuck this up and make you mad, and annoy you, and let you down. But I'm also going to support you, and be your best friend, and help you get everything you want. Success is important but I've been focused on the wrong kind for too long. From now on, the most important success to me is making you the happiest man in the world and making sure that you never regret giving me another chance. I want Epic to rule the world one day but not if it means I can't have you."

Oliver took the last couple of steps that separated us, his hand circling my neck to hold me close. He brushed his lips across my own and I reached out instinctively, wrapping my arms around his waist. His touch was like a balm to my nerves and I felt the tension of the last few days slide away, only to be replaced by his warmth.

"Gareth, give me another chance. Give us another chance. I promise you that you'll never regret it."

I didn't have to think about it. I'd known my decision the minute I'd walked into the bar. I'd known my decision when I'd read his letter. And if I was really honest and dug down deep, my decision had been made three years ago when I'd said yes to this man for the first time.

It wouldn't be the last.

"Yes."

He grinned and then his mouth was on me, his kiss hot and full of promise and wicked intent. His tongue tangled with mine and I moaned into it, desire spiking between us and making us bold and needy. We both forgot that we were in a public bar in the middle of the afternoon.

Catcalls and applause broke us apart. Oliver laughed and waved at the crowd, his final salute aimed at Hank who stood behind the bar shaking his head.

"You wanna get out of here?" Oliver asked, nuzzling his cheek against mine. "Let's go to your place and make love and make plans."

"I like the sound of that, "I answered as we headed towards the door. "First on the agenda is the Smokey Robinson concert next month. I need a date. You have anyone in mind?"

He grinned. "I think I do."

THE END

SHADOW RANCH

Returning to the ranch where your mother killed your father is nobody's idea of fun but Eli Sutherland didn't have anywhere else to go. When the welcome wagon delivers a concussion and a dead body to his farm, sexy Texas Ranger Shep Lockwood is the only good thing about making the move to middle of nowhere Texas.

Chapter One

I wanted to tell the sun to fuck off.

I wanted it to fall out of the sky and plunge into the distant ocean and snuff out like a candle. I also wanted the chirping birds and the cool breeze and all the happy, normal, life-goes-on bullshit things going on around me to just fucking stop while I watched three strangers lower my mother's coffin into the ground.

Just for one goddam minute. Just. Stop.

The heavy fabric of my black, Hugo Boss suit was stifling in the heat of the day, sweat dampening the small of back and my armpits. I didn't move, staring down at the dark cherry coffin with the engraved brass plate.

Nozomi Hayashida. 1966-2016.

I still couldn't believe that my tiny, quiet mother was in that box and I would never see her smile or hear her call me "chan".

And I hated that the last ten years I'd only seen her across the table in the prison visiting room. No physical contact except for a brief hug allowed at the beginning and end of the visit under the watchful eye of the guards.

Life had been fucking unfair to her.

And like any story of tragedy, hers had begun with the choice of the wrong man.

I had a lot in common with my mother besides my looks.

I flinched at the impact of the first clod of dirt on the wood of the coffin. Heavy and empty, it was one of the most final sounds I'd ever heard. It was right up there with the punch of a lover slamming the door behind them and the reverb of a gunshot. This sound was just one more added to my internal personal soundtrack.

I turned away from the scene before me. I couldn't watch this final act of separation, didn't want to. I had enough disturbing shit in my head that I didn't need this visual.

I flinched. I didn't need the visual behind me either.

Bud Sutherland. My uncle. One of my least favorite people on the entire planet. Tall, silver-gray hair and weather beaten skin, he stood tall in his black suit and blacker Stetson.

"Eli," he drawled, "I'm sorry for your loss, son."

He didn't extend his hand. I wouldn't take it anyway.

I bit back the immediate impulse to remind him just whose son I really was, but he knew. Everyone knew that Dutch Sutherland had bastards all over Texas. I was just the one he brought home to rub in the faces of the almighty Sutherland clan.

"I'm just sorry she had to die in prison," I said.

He had enough decency to break eye contact, gazing out over the sea of headstones stretching out behind me. Sutherlands almost as far as the eye could see.

"I know you think I could have done something"

"I know you could and I know you didn't." I stared him down until he made eye contact with me again. "Let's just agree not to bullshit each other and being neighbors won't be so bad."

His eyes narrowed, his lips a thin, tight line of displeasure. "You're staying at Shadow Ranch?"

"For a while."

"I thought you were some big artist in Austin. I think you'll be bored out here."

I laughed and the taste of it was sharp and bitter on my tongue. "You mean you don't want me to stay."

He broke eye contact again. I wondered if my uncle knew he had a tell?

"I just don't think Shadow Ranch is the place for you. I don't know if you'd fit in here."

"What's the real problem? Is it because I'm a bastard? Because my mother killed your brother? My time in the nuthouse or the fact that I sleep with men?" I cocked my head and tapped my chin as if I had to think hard to find the answer. I finally gave him the full brunt of my smile, glad to see the flush of anger on his cheeks. "I'm guessing it's all of the above."

"Ten years has not changed you at all," Bud growled, his hand emerging from the inside of his jacket holding a handkerchief. He wiped at his forehead and then replaced the cloth into the interior pocket. "Come to the house. We need to talk about the ranch."

I watched him walk away, heading towards the dark town car parked on the cemetery road. I hadn't expected anything different from him so I didn't understand the bite of disappointment that clutched at my belly.

"Fucking Sutherlands. Always messing with my head."

Tonight I had a date with a joint and some porn and all would be well again in the morning.

I sucked in a deep breath, inhaling the dry, hot Texas air. It burned going down, obliterating the residual knot of anger and frustration in my belly. All that was left behind was the grief, the loss.

I blinked hard, the moisture on my lashes drying quickly in the heat. Scanning to the right, I noticed the figure standing in the distance. Tall. Male. Strong. All in black including a dark Stetson. Something about him seemed familiar. The way he stood solid and immovable against the backdrop of stone and bright blue sky.

My skin prickled with awareness.

I *knew* him. Or my body was just responding in a primal way to the vision of a virle, living man who walked right out of one of my fantasies. In the face of death, my subconscious was reaffirming that I was taking one breath in and exhaling another one out.

Living.

Surviving.

His hand moved to the brim of his hat and he lifted it slightly, tipping it in a gesture of greeting. A show of respect.

I nodded in acknowledgement, my glance torn away by the noise of the cemetery workers behind me. The small tractor that had been parked in the distance, rumbled towards the gravesite to place the mound of dirt in the grave.

I couldn't watch that.

When I turned back, the mystery cowboy was gone.

Chapter Two

S hadow Ranch was a fine piece of property.

The only thing my father had left me that was worth keeping.

A large main house built of honey-colored wood with a wraparound porch, a faded red door and a large stone fireplace. A smaller house where the residential ranch manager lived and three large barns were surrounded by acres and acres of fenced pasture full of cattle and thoroughbred horses.

It had been years since I'd been here but the man I paid, Kevin Fry, had done a great job. The ranch made money, not a lot, but enough to keep me from selling it. After all that had happened in Austin, I was really glad I hadn't.

Now, I was considering the possibility of making this my permanent home. Leaving Austin and all the shit I'd accumulated there. I was running. Not even gonna lie about it. There was a time when a smart man stood and fought and another when he beat a retreat. I *was* a smart guy in spite of all appearances to the contrary.

I bypassed the barns containing the livestock and headed for the third building, my boots crunching on the pea gravel mix on the pathways. I stopped and looked at the two-story building, the same color as the house with large multi-pane windows on each side of the over-large double doors. It was the only building which might suit as my studio.

I moved forward, sifting through the ring of keys in my hand until I found the one the housekeeper had told me belonged to "the tractor barn" as she called it. Stopping in front of the doors I unlocked them and grabbed one of the large handles, pulling it open with a grunt. They were heavier than they looked.

I stopped and ran a hand down the length of them, admiring the craftsmanship. They were six to eight inches thick and solid. Uncle Bud had only hired the best when he was spending my money. At this moment, I didn't mind.

Stepping into the gloom of the interior, I squinted until I located the light switches and walked over to turn them on. Lights, large and much brighter than I expected, blazed overhead and filled the open space. Concrete floors, a large storage loft overhead and bays along the side housed the two tractors used by the ranch. The middle of the building was open and perfect for my equipment and my artwork.

A quick search of the building proved that the electricity supplied to the building would be sufficient to handle the load of my welding tools and it was outfitted with a sprinkler system. Perfect. It was like the "start-over-and-forget-about-your-shitty-ex" fairy godmother had planned all this out.

I jogged out to the place where my truck was parked and pulled it around to the double doors, backing it up to unload the stuff into the barn. Most of it wasn't so heavy that I couldn't handle it by myself. There were a million and one things to do in the main house but I wasn't quite ready to face all of the memories that pummeled me every time I walked inside so this was at least a productive distraction.

If you *could be* distracted from the memory of when your mother shot your father to death right in front of you.

"Do you need a hand, Mr. Sutherland?"

The deep voice behind me made me jump. I juggled the box of safety equipment in my hands, cringing at the sound of something scraping across the screen of my safety visor. I looked over my shoulder to find Kevin Fry standing behind me in jeans, a ranch logo emblazoned t-shirt and a baseball cap. I glanced back at the large unfinished piece of metalwork I needed to get out of my truck bed and into the barn. It had been a ball buster to get into the truck in Austin and I'd had help. There was no way I was getting it out by myself.

"Sure, Kevin. That would be great." I walked past him and placed the box I held on the ground, groaning when the contents clanked together once again. That visor was fucking pricy and if I'd done a shitty job of packing it in my haste to get out of dodge, I was going to be pissed.

The sun burned my eyes when I ventured back outside, even with my sunglasses on, but I couldn't miss Kevin's confused review of my artwork. Confusion was an improvement over a cold shoulder and veiled hints for me to go back to Austin.

He didn't like me, didn't want me here at all. I got it; he'd been the big man on the ranch for years and my presence was sure to cramp his style. What Kevin failed to realize is that I didn't give a shit.

"Do you like it?" I knew the answer but I couldn't resist asking. The insatiable ego of the artist *had* to know.

"I'm not really sure I know what it is," he ventured cautiously.

I bit back a grin. "Let's get it out of the truck and you can get a better look."

I jumped up into the truck bed and shimmied the piece to the edge on the large moving blanket it was wrapped in. When the cloth was removed the bronze of the metal caught the sunlight, reflecting in sharp arrows aimed towards the sky. Kevin's eyes roamed all over it, flared widely and then shot to meet mine.

He saw it now.

"That's" His voice was strangled, barely making it past his vocal cords to end his thought in a disgust-tinged cough.

"It's two men fucking. I think the mixture of materials and textures add the perfect sense of movement. It's almost as if they're going to emerge from the piece and land right at our feet in living flesh. I'm pleased with it so far."

Sure, I was messing with him. Yeah, I was an asshole. Sue me.

His face was ruddy with his reaction and his jaw clenched tight as he asked, "People buy this stuff?"

"Luckily for me *lots* of people buy this stuff." I nodded towards the end of the piece closest to him. "You want to grab that end and we can get it into the barn."

He reached out for it, barely disguising his revulsion at having to touch it. I rolled my eyes. It wasn't as if I was asking him to recreate the moment captured in the metal with me. I had bad taste in men but I wasn't crazy enough to go after a straight one.

"Kevin," I prompted him again since he continued to stand there and gape at it. I stifled a laugh when he had an erect cock sticking in his face when he finally found the best handhold. "Okay, on the count of three."

He didn't drop it to my amazement and it took only a few moments for the two of us to get it on the space I'd cleared in the middle of the room. We stood up, panting slightly from the exertion of moving a two-hundred pound plus hunk of twisted metal in the middle of a Texas July.

"Are you staying long, Mr. Sutherland?" His question

caught me off-guard, the coldness in his voice didn't. How many times could he ask this question?

"For a little while, Kevin." I turned to look at him, making sure I poured every ounce of unspoken "is that a problem?" into every syllable. "I'd like to sit down with you and go over all of the ranch business and get a tour of the operation as soon as you have the time."

"I'm very busy *running* the ranch," he said, infusing every syllable from his mouth with a "why don't you go back to where you belong" flavor. Pretty gutsy to get shitty with the guy who paid the bills.

"Well, then *tomorrow* would be great, Kevin. I'll be in your office at one."

He stared. I stared back. Poor Kevin had no idea that after two years with Neal I was a pro at dealing with sullen, childish men.

"I'm doing a good job at Shadow Ranch," he bit out.

"And I never said you weren't. I just want to know what I'm paying for around here. I think it's about time, don't you?" I glanced down at my watch. "I've got to pick up some things for the house. Thanks for your help."

"You pay me to do it," he answered, not even trying to disguise his irritation.

I leveled my gaze at him, wondering just how much trouble he was going to be for me. A lot, if the mulish set of his jaw was any indicator. But, the one thing two years with my ex-lover had taught me was how to deal with troublemakers, so Mr. Fry was in for a rude awakening. I gave him my biggest smile and a sexy wink just to bust his balls. "Yes, I do."

Chapter Three

Harry's Stop-n-Shop Bar and Feed Store was a place everyone should go once.

You'd think that the smell of animal feed, day-old popcorn and over-done microwave burritos would turn people off but you'd be wrong. Every Friday and Saturday night, people showed up in their best party wear to line dance, eat wings, and drink cheap draft beer. When I was a teenager we could always con somebody into buying us beer and then we'd hang out in the back parking lot and smoke pot and get laid.

Well, other people got laid. I got high.

I spent most of my time hiding the fact that it wasn't the cheerleaders, but the quarterback, who got my dick hard and figuring out inventive ways to avoid going home. I wouldn't go back to high school for a million dollars.

I walked into the Stop-n-Shop portion of the building and grabbed one of the mini-carts from the front. Milk, eggs, bread, lunch meat, fruits, veggies, some stuff to make for quick suppers and beer were the things I needed. "In and out" was the goal because I wanted to get my equipment set up tonight so that I could work on my piece tomorrow.

I was so used to ordering in from the million takeout places near my place that I wandered down the first few aisles like a man who'd grown up in Amish territory. I was so overwhelmed by the sheer range of choice that I just started throwing random crap in my cart. Way too many items later I rolled up to the cashier and started flinging stuff onto the belt.

"How're you doing today sir?" The perky woman dressed in the red and white gingham uniform asked.

"Fine" I lifted a can of peaches in syrup and wondered if I'd ever liked to eat them. No idea. I flung them on the belt anyway, "I guess."

She held up a blue box of mac and cheese. "You know these are five for five dollars, right? If you want me to go ahead and ring you up for five, you can go back and get the other fourwell, holy shit."

Her use of what I guessed was not proper language for an employee of Harry's Stop-n-Shop Bar and Feed Store stopped me in mid-fling. I looked up and she was staring at me, mouth hanging slightly open and I wondered what the hell was wrong with my face. I resisted the urge to reach up and confirm that everything was where it should be.

"Eli Sutherland, what in the world are you doing here?" She practically yelled at me across the counter, her body vibrating with excitement. I took a step back for my own safety just in case she launched in my direction.

I took a good, long look at her face and something started triggering recognition deep in my brain.

"Don't strain yourself trying to figure it out. I lost thirty pounds on Weight Watchers and I dyed my hair," she patted the red curls on her head and smiled. "It's Marnie Stokes, well Marnie Taylor now. I married Darren Taylor who was a year ahead of us at school. You probably don't remember him."

Oh yeah. Marnie Stokes. We'd sat near each other in homeroom from kindergarten to the day I was shipped off to the "special school for kids with emotional problems because their mom blew their abusive dad to kingdom come in the living room". She'd been a good friend to me and I'd *almost* told her I was gay.

That should have been enough to keep us close for the rest of our lives. Or at least until graduation.

I smiled at her. "Yeah, Marnie. It's good to see you." I searched for what else to say. "Congrats on getting married and the weight loss."

I cringed at the last part. I blamed it on my level of hunger. I knew better than to talk about a woman's weight even if she brought it up.

"Well, you're just as sweet as you ever were," she said as she started scanning my items and dropping them into bags. "Handsome too. You bring a boyfriend or a husband with you?"

"Uh, no. Neither one," I mumbled as I stacked filled bags in my cart.

"Well, then you need to make sure you come out here on Saturday night. *Everyone* comes to Harry's on Saturday night. I'll be here with Darren and a lot of the old crowd and they'd love to see you. There's no reason for you to sit out on that ranch all by yourself."

I didn't know what "old crowd" she was talking about. I'd been a loner, gay and an artist. While everyone else wore Wranglers and cowboy hats, I'd worn David Bowie and Sex Pistols t-shirts, eyeliner and a shitty attitude.

"I don't know," I hedged. Sitting at home by myself and working was *exactly* my plan.

"I'll come out there and get you if we don't see you. I promise you I will."

Something about her told me she would and so I just nodded and decided to figure out a way to get out of it by Saturday or to suck it up, drive into town, and get a beer. It wasn't like there would be anyone to cruise. As far as I knew I was the only gay guy in the county.

She finished ringing up my stuff and I swiped my card and declined a receipt. And then I stood there mute as she rounded the counter and grabbed me in a huge hug. I flailed, unsure about where to put my hands or if I wanted to. And then she delivered the whammy.

"I'm so sorry about your mama," she whispered against my neck.

Before I knew I was doing it, my arms wrapped around her and I returned the hug with everything I had. It felt good and I realized that it was the first time I'd been touched since I'd left Austin besides a brief handshake from the funeral director. I sank into it, letting the feeling wash over me and all the sounds of the Stop-n-Shop went away.

Once upon a time I'd been a man who hugged and touched and connected with other people but the last year with Neal had stripped me of that. It felt too vulnerable, too needy and I'd convinced myself that I didn't need it. Fuck, I'd been wrong and for the first time I felt like maybe I wasn't just running from Austin but to something I needed from Shadow Ranch.

I pulled away before I drifted too far into my Oprah moment but not before we'd gotten a couple of strange looks from shoppers. She released me and brushed away wetness on her cheek before turning the smile on to its full wattage.

"I mean it. Drinks here at 7:30 or I'll be at Shadow Ranch at eight."

"I'll be there," I said before I could stop myself and I knew I'd regret my agreement a million times between the minute I walked into the parking lot until Saturday night.

I drove home to the ranch, running over and over the complete unexpectedness of the entire encounter at the store. One trip to get eggs and a good chunk of what I planned about this trip had been sidelined by reconnecting with people I'd known before it had all gone to hell. Was I staying? Was I only here long enough to get my feet back under me?

Shit if I knew anymore.

My crazy circle of thoughts kept me occupied all the way back to the ranch. I raced the sunset, arriving in my front drive just as the fire of the sun licked at the horizon. I slid out of the truck cab and stood there, gawking at the beauty of the sky as it sank into indigo, purple and then inky blue. We didn't get sunsets like this in Austin.

I hustled to get my groceries put away and decided to walk over to the horse barn to see them all put up in their stalls. I was starving but it could a wait a few minutes longer since I now planned to eat, smoke a joint and settle in for a nice night with some of my favorite porn.

Who needed Harry's Stop-n-Shop Bar and Feed Store when I had MaryJane, wifi and unlimited streaming?

I headed out across the driveway, the pea gravel crunching under my boots. My flashlight was too small to give me much help in finding my way so I was glad for the automatic lights installed along the ledges of some of the buildings. The land beyond them was complete darkness but at least I wouldn't stumble over anything immediately in front of me.

I rounded the corner of the breezeway barn and peered inside, listening for huffing sounds of the horses as they settled in. I'd always loved that sound. For me it was like that moment when you sink into your bed after a long day and you let the cocoon of pillows and sheets envelope you. Heaven.

The sharp spark of pain in the back of my head was more like hell. My eyes watered, my ears rang and I cried out. Horses startled around me and I pitched forward, the second blow glancing off my shoulder instead of my skull and throwing me to the ground as everything went black.

Chapter Four

I woke in my second least favorite place on the earth: a hospital.

The place that held the number one spot for me was the "New Beginnings School for Troubled Youth". Don't let the name fool you; pretty words can make any prison appear to be a palace. I'd passed my two years of incarceration navigating the haze of above and below the table drugs and getting my ass kicked by kids who didn't like the fact that I was gay or the son of a convicted murderer or both. Life in Texas isn't all "Friday Night Lights."

But this looked like a legitimate medical facility. White and bright with people dressed in scrubs and machines beeping on either side of me so loudly that I thought my head was going to fall off. I tried to sit up and the unholy pounding inside my skull quickly pointed out to me that it was a very bad idea.

The voice from the direction of the doorway seconded that motion.

"I wouldn't try to sit up. They say you have a nasty concussion."

I slid one eye open and located the owner of the sexy, deep

drawl. Leaning against the doorframe, he was bulky enough to make me feel small. I'm tall and muscular from spending hours lifting and manipulating large pieces of heavy metal but I'm lanky, built more like my Japanese ancestors than my Texas forebears. This guy looked like he could support the entire weight of the hospital on his shoulders and not break a sweat.

I'd bet my welding equipment that *he'd* played football in high school.

He moved into the room and I spied the badge hooked to his waistband. A silver star.

"Mr. Sutherland, I'm Ranger Shepherd Lockwood. I'm here to investigate the attack on you earlier this evening."

What time was it? I turned my head to find a clock and the spike of pain behind my eyes left me sweaty and nauseated. I hurt all over, mostly down my right side. I blearily remembered the floor of the barn coming up to meet my face. Thank God I didn't remember the impact.

"You need to take it easy, Mr. Sutherland. Here, see if you can keep some water down."

I felt the warm touch of his hand on my shoulder and I pried one eye open enough to see him waving a paper cup under my chin. I took a sip, waited to see if I was going to impersonate Linda Blair and when I only got a vague rumble, took another. It was cool and wonderful and I sighed in relief as I leaned back on the pillow.

"I've been bashed on the head enough to know that moving right now isn't a good idea," he said, his voice tinted with laughter.

My lips twitched up into a slight smile in spite of the pain. "Let me guess—quarterback?"

"Wide receiver," he chuckled and I looked up to find him very close. His eyes were grey, a color matched by the strands of matching pewter in his dark hair. My breath stuttered setting off the robotic beep of my monitor in an erratic rhythm and giving me away.

If Ranger Lockwood didn't know I was gay, he did now. Outed by medical equipment.

His gaze slid over to it and when he looked back at me, there was laughter but also something very close to interest in his eyes. Or it was the drugs making me see shit that wasn't there.

I definitely had a type. Big, solid, dark hair with just enough scruff to make you feel them the morning after in the best places. My gaze slid over to where his light tan Stetson perched on the coat hooks on the wall by the door. I liked a man in a cowboy hat. Yes, I did.

I looked at it again. Wait a minute. I'd seen that hat before.

"You were at my mother's funeral," I said and then an even more distant memory emerged. "Ranger Lockwood, you were there the night"

He moved away from me and pulled over one of the two chairs in the room, settling in before returning my gaze. The humor and spark from just a few moments earlier were gone, replaced with sympathy. Not pity, thank God. That would have pissed me off. No, it was just understanding of what that had all meant to a sixteen year old with no one to rely on.

"Call me Shep," he cleared his throat and I realized that he was nervous about how to go on. It eased the knot in my gut just enough to make breathing a little easier. "I was a Sheriff's Deputy at the time. Second officer on the scene. My first murder. You were just a kid."

Memories flooded back and I winced at the physical pain that came along with them. After all this time. And yes, I did remember him.

"You were the one that placed the plastic bags over my hands," I murmured. "So they could determine if I was the one who killed my father."

"You didn't."

"No, I just brought the shotgun out to begin with and set the whole nightmare in motion."

"Your father was beating your mother. You brought the gun out"

"To kill him," I answered. No sense in denying the truth. It was in multiple police reports and court testimony.

"But. You. Didn't."

I sighed and looked at him. "So, is that why you're here?"

"No," he looked down, pulling a small notebook and pen out of his jacket pocket. "Your uncle called and asked us to look into your attack, Mr. Sutherland.

I resisted the urge to roll my eyes "Good old Uncle Bud. Exerting his influence everywhere he can." I paused. "And call me Eli."

He nodded. "I'm surprised he's not here."

I snorted. "That's why he sent you."

My obvious derision filled the air with a downer that I hadn't intended. Crap. In spite of the topic, I'd been enjoying the conversation with the hot-as-fuck man of the law.

"So, who knocked me over the head and why?" I asked.

"I was hoping you knew," Shep answered, clicking the end of his ballpoint and scribbling on his paper. When he looked back up at me he was all cop. Eyes darkened to the color of steel and mouth grim. "Did you hear or see anyone?"

"Nobody. I went out to look at the horses and then saw fireworks as someone clocked me from behind."

"You've been gone a long time. Why did you come back to the ranch?"

This. How much did I tell? All of it. If he was any good at his job, he'd find out anyway.

"My boyfriend was stealing me blind and sleeping with my agent so I ditched them both and decided to come to the ranch for a while to get my shit together."

He blinked. Long and slow. No reaction on his face in spite of the big gay drama I'd just verbally vomited all over him. His response was low and even.

"How's that working out for you?"

"I'm lying in a hospital bed with my ass hanging out of the back of this gown. How does it look like I'm doing?"

He stared at me for a moment and then glanced down, writing while he continued his questioning. "Do you think your ex and your agent could have done this?"

I tried to picture Neal doing anything that required *actual work* and failed.

"No. Neal is too lazy to try to kill me and Alec hopes to get me back as a client. I made him a shit ton of money."

"They're not together?" His forehead crinkled in confusion.

"No." I chuckled and it sounded as mean as I felt about the whole situation. "Neal was cheating on him too."

I could almost hear Shep rolling around the evidence of my shitty taste in lover and agent in the silence.

"So, anyone *local* who might want to knock you out?" He said, moving on to a new topic.

"My uncle, any of the Sutherlands. My ranch manager, Kevin Fry," I rattled off the names of the people I knew didn't want me to stick around very long.

He scribbled the names down and shook his head. "You've only been here two days, that's fast work." He grinned and my monitors gave a treacherous blip once again. Shep Lockwood got to me and I wanted to lock him in my studio, strip him down and sculpt every hard, honed inch of him.

Steel. He would need steel.

He was staring at me, pen poised in the air, his smile slipping into something sultrier. Busted. I let my own mouth tip into a half grin before looking away and continuing.

"With my uncle it's been twenty-six years in the making. The rest of the clanthey never accepted me or my mother."

"Never helped you either," he murmured and I cut my gaze back to his. There was that sympathy again. Damn it all, for being so appealing. "I was new to the area when your father was killed. It's my understanding that everyone knew what was going on in your house but nobody stepped in and tried to help."

"That's right. Nobody did." I let the anger roll through me, the adrenaline spike dulling the pain for a bit. I moved on from the old news, stewing over it wouldn't change it. "Kevin Fry doesn't want me interfering with his job at the ranch. He's made it clear that he doesn't want me here" I paused at the next part and then decided that it *might* be relevant. "and he doesn't like the fact that I'm gay."

Shep nodded, not even sparing me a blink for that information. "Are you planning on staying? "

"I don't know how long I'll be here. It might be permanent. I might just spend part of the year here. I still have my gallery in Austin, my apartment" I shrugged. "I have no definite plans."

"Maybe he's afraid you'll find something worth staying for," he said, gaze locked on mine.

I stared back. The temperature in the chilly room spiked up about twenty degrees and I was glad I had a blanket covering my hardening cock. It was bad enough I had the monitor going off again like a drummer on a Red Bull.

I cleared my throat. "Maybe, I will."

Shep closed his notebook and rose to his feet. "There's a lot to like about this place. Lot's of nice people" he gave a small laugh. "who won't try to kill you."

"That would be a plus." I paused before blurting out. "I've been invited out for drinks at Harry's Saturday night by an old classmate, Marnie Taylor."

"Everyone goes to Harry's on Saturday night."

"That's what she said."

"She's right." He shoved his notebook into his jacket pocket and when he brought out his hand, there was a card in it. "This has all my contact information, my cell number is on the back. Call if you think of anything else or if you need anything."

I took it from him, running a finger over the raised lettering and the seal of the Texas Rangers.

"I'll call if I think of anything."

He grabbed his hat off the wall peg and nodded to me. "Get some rest."

I watched him go and wondered if Shep would be at Harry's on Saturday night.

Chapter Five

Y ou could hear the country music in the parking lot.

The sound pouring out of Harry's Stop-n-Shop Bar and Feed Store reverberated in my head, which still ached a little from my bashing two days earlier. It was bearable though and I even had a jump of excitement in my belly at the prospect of going out and being with people again. After years of living in the heart of Austin, the solitude of the ranch wasn't a tight fit for me anymore. I liked the quiet space to work but it did get lonely out there.

The blast of sound hit me like a stiff Texas wind when I opened the door and I grinned. I didn't know the exact song but country music was a favorite of mine. Nobody could paint a picture of an emotional trainwreck and still entice you to jump on it and ride like a country songwriter. As a fellow artist, I could appreciate the talent.

The large room was dim but my eyes adjusted quickly and the vision of fifty people line-dancing filled my view. Men and women of all ages and ethnicity were strutting their collective stuff in perfect synchronicity. I leaned over the bar and shouted my request for a ginger ale, the doctor having sworn me off alcohol for a couple more days. I didn't mind, I was my own designated driver tonight and for the foreseeable future.

"Eli!"

I heard her before I felt her tackle me from behind and it was only luck that kept me from spilling my entire drink all over the bar. I turned to find Marnie grinning from ear-to-ear with a gleam in her eye that made me nervous.

"I was getting ready to send Darren out to the ranch to get you." She grabbed my arm and dragged me over to a table full of men and women smiling at me with way too much expectation. Introductions were made but I couldn't have told you half of them if my life depended on it. Some of them I recognized from high school and I figured they were the "old crowd" Marnie had talked about.

One face I did recognize though.

Ranger Shep Lockwood looked as good in a dark blue shirt and jeans with a little bit of scruff as he did clean-shaven in his Ranger's uniform. Fuck me.

My skin flushed hot and my heart did that stupid skipping thing it had done in the hospital. My cock pulsed with interest and I shifted to allow some extra room in my jeans.

I nodded at him and he raised his beer in salute.

"Eli, put that drink down and come on out and dance with me," Marnie yelled over the music.

I shook my head. "I don't know this one. I'm not much of a dancer."

"Come on out here and shake that fine ass," She tugged me out with her, surprisingly strong. "You can't tell me you spent all that time in Austin and didn't learn to dance."

"That's exactly what I'm saying."

"You're lying," she laughed.

"Don't say I didn't warn you."

She ignored my comment and drew me into the line with her, holding my hand as she walked me through the steps. I stumbled around, banging into Marnie and the woman on the other side of me. They laughed and prodded me into the correct steps and I followed along as best I could without causing anyone permanent damage. It must have been an extended mix because it was the longest damn song I'd ever heard.

I looked up and caught Shep watching me, his eyes filled with laughter even though he did a great job of keeping the smile edging his mouth under control. When he couldn't contain it any longer he snickered, lifted his bottle and took a sip of beer. I flipped him the bird and he raised an eyebrow in response.

"So, you met Shep?" Marnie asked, nudging me in the ribs. She smiled and I could see the matchmaking hamster running at top speed in the wheel in her brain. "You know, he's gay too. You guys should go out."

"Just because we're both gay doesn't mean that we're automatically attracted to each other, Marnie," I shouted over the music.

"Yeah, I know that you idiot." She gave my arm a shove this time and an eyeroll. "Darren used to watch me dance the way Shep is watching you. That's all I'm saying."

I glanced back at him and he *was* looking at me, watching me as he spoke to a couple still seated at the table. When our eyes locked, he stared, his gaze raking over me from the top of my head to the scuffed bottoms of my boots. He ate me up, devouring me from a distance and I felt every bit of it; along my skin, my gut, the rush of my blood in my veins. Flushed and distracted I messed up the next couple of steps and the dance forced me to look away or risk a trip and fall. He didn't break the contact until I did and then I turned to face Marnie and her knowing smirk.

The longest song in the world finally ended and when she tried to keep me out there for the next one I waved her off. I headed back to table, reaching out for my drink as Shep pushed it in my direction. He motioned to the open seat next to him and I took it.

He turned his body towards me and leaned in closer to talk, his arm draped along the back of my chair. When I leaned backwards and pressed against him, we locked gazes and traded smiles. I liked that he didn't play games. After Neal, it was nice, simple.

"Nice job out there," Shep said, still trying to bite back his grin.

"I *told* Marnie I wasn't a very good dancer."

"Well, then she was warned. You didn't lie."

I paused with my glass in mid-air at his words, so close to my own. "You're a shit, Ranger Lockwood."

"You're not the first one to say it."

That was interesting. The first black mark on the seemingly perfect Ranger.

"So, you have a Neal or two in your background too?" I took a sip of my ginger ale and debated my next question. "Or were *you* the Neal?"

He lifted his own bottle, hesitating before taking a drink and then answering coolly and without any heat. "No, I was never the cheater but I've been on the receiving end. When you get to my age " he shrugged, "It happens. It sucks but it happens."

Silence dragged out between us but it wasn't uncomfortable as we stared at each other, drinking our drinks and ignoring all the noise and bustle around us.

"You look good," Shep finally said.

"Oh, don't back down now. I think we covered how dumb I looked out there on the dance floor," I answered, signaling the waitress for another ginger ale as I turned to sit my empty glass on the table.

"No. That's not what I just said," he insisted, leaning in

very close to me, his breath hot on my cheek. "I said you look good. Now." His leg nudged against me with purpose and I followed his unspoken order and returned my gaze to his. "You even looked good to me in that hospital bed, Eli. I *like* how you look."

Fuck. My cock fought against the confines of my jeans because everything he was doing was turning me on. Shep Lockwood knew where my buttons were and exactly how to push them.

"I like how you say what you want," I answered, licking my lips, my heart pausing as I watched his pupils dilate as his gaze followed the path of my tongue. I didn't know this guy but what I did know appealed to me and he was hot, smokin'. Two men, attracted to each other and unattached. I decided to go for broke. "I'll return the favor."

"Yeah?" he asked.

I shifted forward dropping my hand to brush my fingers overs his muscled forearm, letting the dark hair tickle the end of my fingers. He was hot to the touch, alive and vibrant with the restraint I could see was holding him in his chair.

"I like how you look at me," I breathed.

"How's that?" He asked, his voice catching a little on the second word, his breathing faster, hotter against my skin. "How do I look at you?"

"Like you want to eat me alive."

"I'd love to know what you taste like, Eli Sutherland. That's the truth."

He could be lying to me. I didn't care. Not tonight.

Shep placed his beer bottle on the table and then reached down, his long fingers sweeping over the inside of my wrist and across my palm. It was slow, seductive and I followed his lead. He was the Pied Piper and I would go where he wanted.

"Come on."

We left the table, winding in between the bodies and the

bar staff, headed towards the outside of the building. No one gave us a second look, at least not one I could tell. I hated that I felt like I had to check but I was unfamiliar with this terrain. In Austin, I knew where I could go and not be hassled by people but this was a whole new world. I trusted Shep to know the natives, to know if this was safe, and when the warm, night air hit my face I leaned into the arm he looped around my waist.

I let him take the lead across the lot, only a few people dotted the space and he nodded or threw a wave at everyone he saw.

He didn't stop, didn't slow down our brisk pace until we turned a corner to the darker side of the lot and he pushed me against a large, black truck. I wondered if it was his for a brief second before I spied his familiar Stetson on the dashboard and then I saw nothing but Shep as he filled up the space between us with his large, hard body.

"Just a taste." He murmured and then it was warm lips pressed against mine and the insistent sweep of his tongue.

He tasted like his beer and a long-distant mint and I opened my mouth to him as I slipped my arms around his neck and pulled him even closer. Shep's large hands grabbed my ass, bringing our groins into friction-filled contact that made me groan out loud. My cock lengthened in my jeans and I strained to get closer to him, to increase the pressure.

He bent his knees a little to make up for the slight difference in our height, arched up and the perfect contact made us break apart on a gasp of pleasure and want. I leaned back and found his eyes, dark and stormy now with the black dilation of his pupils and full of only one question: "How far do you want this to go?"

I had the answer.

"Move back a little," I said, lowering my hands to insert

them between us. He did as he was told and then it was my job to unfasten belts and buttons, and lower zippers.

His cock was thick and fat and I traced the heavy vein that ran along its underside with my thumb. I gave him a long, slow stroke that wrung a deep, guttural moan from his mouth.

"Yes, fucking touch me, Eli. Please."

Gone was the in-control, steady Texas Ranger and in his place was a needy man who greedily watched as he thrust into the hot grip of my hand. A bead of pre-cum sat on the fat, purple head and I caught it in my palm, using it to aid my glide up and down his shaft.

His large, warm hand found my own cock and he pumped me, his other trailing lower to grip my balls, kneading them gently in time with his rhythm. We leaned our foreheads together, both watching, breathing harsh and labored in the relative still of the evening air, the thud of the music and laughter of the bar patrons far, far away.

Shep rubbed his thumb just under the head of my cock, my most sensitive spot and I came up on my toes, chasing his grip with my hungry need.

"I want to come so bad," I panted, dipping down to capture his mouth in a quick, dirty, wet kiss. My body arched, my groin thrusting towards him as if he didn't know that I needed his touch exactly where it was. "Make me come, Shep."

"Look at me," he demanded and I did, my head snapping back to hit the glass of his driver's side window with a thud. It hurt but the sharp only intensified the sweet fire rising up from my balls.

I came. Hot and wet, rolling down over his fist and spattering against the exposed part of my belly. The scent, salty and earthy, filled the space between us as he leaned in to take my mouth and my cry.

"Fucking beautiful." He dove in deep with his tongue,

possession and desperation in his taste. Almost as soon as it began, the kiss was over and he was looking at me, his face open and vulnerable. "You're so goddam beautiful."

I gave him a long, hard stroke and nipped at his lower lip and he came, his moan loud and guttural. I stared at him, soaking in the way his rock-hewn features softened with his pleasure, how he gave it all with no hesitation. As if he'd never been hurt or he trusted me enough to let me in. He was gorgeous, lips swollen with our kisses, eyes dazed with the endorphins of a good jack-off session with someone you liked.

Leaning forward, I took his mouth this time and swept his warmth with my tongue, coaxing him down from the high with the promise of more. Like a pusher who gives out the first one for free, I wanted him hooked and back for more.

I didn't know how long I was staying but while I was here, I wanted as much of Shep Lockwood as I could get. He was too good to pass up. He must have read my mind.

"I know you're nothing but trouble Eli, but I can't seem to help myself."

His accent was more pronounced, the orgasm-induced drawl making me shiver. All I wanted at this point was to keep him talking.

"The good kind or the bad kind?" I asked, lifting my head to allow him to trace my neck with sexy bites and teasing licks.

His laugh rumbled in his chest, his breath causing goose-bumps to form on my skin. Shep pulled back and looked at me, his eyes sultry in the moonlight.

"The best kind is always a little bit of both."

Chapter Six

I knew exactly what a gunshot sounded like.

One minuted I'd been dreaming of Shep. In my bed. My cock in his hot, wet mouth.

The next, I'd heard a sound I'd never forget.

Real or in my worst nightmares, I'd know that sound anywhere and one had just cut through the silent air of the ranch. The second one shook me completely out of my sleep stupor. It sounded like it was coming from the ranch manager's house.

I leapt out of bed and grabbed the nearest pair of jeans off my floor, threw a t-shirt on and shoved my bare feet into my boots. I ran to the front door and paused long enough to grab my cellphone and to consider taking a gun. I had one but it wasn't loaded and I hadn't handled one in a very long time. There was already one gun too many in this equation.

Deciding against it, I burst out the front door of the ranch house and bolted across the property towards the manager's place. It was the dark of a few hours after midnight, the long expanse of drive only lit by the solar lights marking the edges so I didn't see the truck barreling in my direction. Lights off and a dark paint color, the rumble of the engine was my only warning to jump out of the way.

Pea gravel scraped against the bare skin of my palms and arms and I cried out. My abused body screamed out silently and I wondered just how much more I could take before something got seriously damaged. I rolled to the side and squinted at the retreating truck, trying to make out the license plate as it sped away. It didn't look like a ranch truck, the wrong make and model, but I couldn't be sure.

It didn't matter. The gunshot was disturbing enough but the combination of it with the late-night angry driver made me get to my feet and run faster to the manager's house.

The door to the house was wide open, light streaming into bright rectangles onto the porch and the driveway. I took the steps two at a time.

"Kevin! It's Eli. Are you okay?" I yelled out, my voice bouncing back to me in the stillness. I wasn't familiar with the layout but it didn't take long to find him in the kitchen. On the floor. A rapidly growing pool of blood under him.

I stopped on a dime, the shock of the scene before me so familiar. So ugly. So terrifying.

It wasn't my father on the floor this time, I knew it. My brain understood that it was a different time and a different place but the slickness in my armpits and on my back betrayed my visceral reaction. The tang of blood in the air was so thick I choked on it, biting back the rise of bile in my throat. I was frozen.

Until he moaned.

It was a gurgle of blood that rumbled up from his chest and dribbled out between his lips and down his chin. There wasn't a lot of it because most of his blood was seeping and spurting out of the two big holes in his gut.

It was disgusting, horrifying. It was enough to get my ass moving.

I slid in the pool of blood, dropping to my knees beside his body. I ignored the rapidly cooling wetness soaking into my jeans.

Reaching over my shoulder, I grabbed a handful of my t-shirt and dragged it over my head, bunching it together and pressing down over the wounds.

"Fuck. Fuck." Kevin's rose up, back arching in pain as he tried to scream past the blood and the gore. "Goddam. Just be still. I'm calling for help."

I leaned down, keeping one hand pressed against his abdomen while I reached around and slid my phone from the back pocket of my jeans. It fell to the ground, sliding from my bloody fingers and I had to lunge for it. I jostled Kevin and blood spurted through the t-shirt and my fingers.

"Fuck." I reached for the phone again and with trembling fingers dialed "911". "This is Shadow Ranch. Someone's been shot. Send someone"

I broke off my plea when the sounds of sirens cut through the night and screamed just outside the front door of the house. I could see the red and blue lights shining through the open door and reflecting off the walls and the photographs.

I threw the phone down and yelled, "Back here! In the kitchen."

Heavy booted footsteps pounded down the hallway towards me and before I knew it the doorway filled with policemen, serious and guns drawn.

"Put your hands up!"

They all shouted at me at the same time, the same thing, guns pointed at my head. I glanced down at Kevin.

"I'm trying to keep pressure"

"Get your hands up in the air now." The last guy sounded like he meant business so I did as I was told, taking my hands off Kevin's chest.

They swarmed me and I was yanked up onto my feet,

manhandled as rough hands searched me for weapons. Leaving the gun at home had been the best idea ever.

Paramedics poured in and descended on Kevin, barking orders at each other while the officer behind me slammed a pair of cuffs on my wrists.

"What the fuck?" I tried to twist around but he was huge and determined. "I didn't do anything. I called you guys."

"Are you Eli Sutherland?"

I nodded.

"Somebody called it in and said you shot Kevin Fry."

A large familiar body filled the doorway and I turned, relief coursing through my body at the sight of Shep. He swept the room and several of the officers stopped what they were doing, clearly looking to him for whatever came next.

I hoped it wasn't keeping me in the handcuffs. Or sending me to prison for a crime I didn't commit.

"Shep, get me out of these cuffs," I pleaded.

He walked over to me, his eyes the color of steel with a voice to match. "Eli Sutherland we are taking you in for questioning in the attempted murder of Kevin Fry."

Chapter Seven

I hate police stations.

I don't think this makes me unique but being in lockup makes me twitchy for things I gave up a long time ago because I didn't want to be predictable. Or dead.

I'd been dumped in here over an hour ago. Or longer. I had no idea. There was no clock, I didn't have my watch, and they'd confiscated my blood soaked phone.

My clothes were gone and the pair of sweats they'd given me smelled of too much bleach and scratched my bare ass. My hands were raw from scrubbing off the chemicals they used to check me for gun residue and Kevin's blood. I had no idea if he was okay or not. I had no idea if I was okay.

I knew nothing.

Questioned, I told him what little I knew. And then I'd told them again. And again. I still knew nothing.

The two-way glass gave me no answers. Solid and blank. I didn't even know if anyone was behind it.

I wanted Shep.

The door opened and he came in as if I'd conjured him out of wishes and my prayers. I was so relieved I barely noticed the uniformed police officer who slipped in beside him and stationed himself at the door.

"Is Kevin okay?" I asked, rising to my feet before I remembered that I was chained to the table. The metal links rattled and I tumbled back onto the hard metal chair, wincing when my bruises hit the seat and the straight back.

"Unchain him," Shep said, easing into the chair opposite mine. I watched him as the police officer walked around the room and unlocked my handcuffs, unwinding the chain and setting me free. Well, as free as I was going to get detained in a police station. Shep continued to look down at the tabletop, rifling through the pages of his open file. When the officer completed his task Shep murmured, "Leave us alone, please."

The door closed behind the officer with a soft click and there was silence in the air between us. I waited. There was nothing else I could do. I didn't know if I was dealing with Shep or Ranger Lockwood. It was like the man who'd touched me, who'd laughed with me over the ridiculousness of jerking each other off in parking lot like a couple of teenagers was long gone.

I waited.

He looked up at me.

"Kevin Fry is dead," His voice was even, low. I still couldn't read him.

"Oh God," I whispered, slumping back into the chair, rubbing my hand over my cheek, my chin, my eyes. My palm rasped against what little stubble I had and I shut my eyes against the rise of emotion in my chest. I wasn't sure if it was grief for a man I didn't know or fear for myself. Maybe a little of both. I opened my eyes and stared at Shep, ensuring that I had his complete attention. "I didn't kill him."

Beats passed and I held my breath.

"I know," he said, huffing out an exhausted sigh before leaning forward and mimicking my movements of moments before. "No residue on your hands. The timing of the first 911 call was all off. Nothing about this adds up to you being the shooter but somebody wanted to set you up." I watched as he rubbed his eyes and then ran his fingers through the thick brush of his dark hair. His eyes were a stormy pewter when he met mine again. "I think you're in the middle of something that might get you killed."

"Jesus, Shep. I just got here."

"And I think your arrival has caused these problems."

"So what am I supposed to do about it?" I pointed at him. "You're the police. You do something about it."

"That's what I intend to do," he stated, his tone firm as he flipped through the pages in the file. "You didn't get any part of the license plate? The make or model?"

I shook my head. I told him the same thing I told the other officers. "It was dark and I was freaked out from almost getting run over. I know it wasn't the kind of truck we have at the ranch. We have all Ford vehicles."

"That's something." He looked at me. "No strange people hanging around the ranch? People who didn't belong there?"

"I'm a stranger there. I wouldn't know who should be there and who shouldn't."

"Fair enough." Shep paused and I could see he was rolling something over his mind. I braced myself for something I wouldn't like. "Could I persuade you to leave the ranch for a while?"

I shook my head.

He leaned in close across the table, not reaching out to touch me but I could tell he wanted to. Hell, I wanted him to do it.

"I don't want you to be the next person I find dead at Shadow Ranch, Eli." Shep's voice was low, reminiscent of the one he used last night at Harry's. It was intimate, direct. "Especially not you."

117

I licked my lips. My heart did a hard thud in my chest and I told myself not to jump too far into this, to not want what he was offering too much. I liked him but I still didn't know if I was going to stay or if I was headed right back to Austin.

"I don't want to be the next dead body you find either," I said, lifting my lips in a half smile. "I'm still looking for something worth staying for."

The tension in the room broke and he leaned over again, laughing slightly as he rubbed his face again. When he looked back at me, he shook his head like he was doing something really crazy.

"Fine, then I'll be staying at the ranch with you."

Chapter Eight

"This is a great house," Shep said, his gaze sweeping all over the room as he dumped his overnight bag on the floor.

I mimicked him and looked around the large central room of the ranch house trying to see what he saw. Stone fireplace surrounded by comfortable leather furniture, honeyed wood floors and an updated kitchen that somebody on the cooking shows I never watch would love to have. I wasn't much of a cook. Neal had taken on that duty during the days when he'd tried to please me, when he tried to give the impression that we were partners.

I'd mistaken a full belly for a full life. Shame on me.

"Do you like it?"

He turned to me, his smile quizzical. "And you don't?"

"I have such a mix of good and bad memories here." My eyes drifted towards the place near the large front window, the place where the floorboards were a little darker in appearance. They were newer, replacing the ones covered in the blood of my father.

I looked back at Shep, finding his gaze focused on me. His

eyes were more gray than blue in the dim interior but they were clear, open. Everything about him screamed "this is a guy you can trust" and almost every part of me wanted to run from what I saw there. What I thought I might want, might need.

He broke eye contact first but not before I caught the smile that lifted the corner of his mouth. He shouldered past me and walked with purpose to the fridge, opened it and peered inside. I watched him, admiring the shape of his fine ass sticking out beyond the edge of the door. When he stood up and I lost sight of the view, only my curiosity kept me from asking him to resume his position.

"I suggest that you replace the bad memories with new ones, better ones."

He was grinning at me and I could help but smile right back. "And you think my future good memories are in my fridge?"

"The ingredients of the supper I will make for you are in the fridge and in my vast life experience I know that nobody can make good memories without a hot shower and a good meal," he said with friendly sarcasm.

Fuck but that sounded good.

Shep looked smug. "I can tell by the look on your face that you agree with me so get your ass in the shower and I'll cook."

I knew better than to argue. A hot man in my kitchen offering to cook for me after the shit day I'd had? Sold.

———

THE ONLY REASON I got out of the shower was because I was starving.

Standing under the spray, dialed up as hot as I could stand it for twenty minutes brought on the shakes and I held on to the edge of the sink to prevent myself from face-planting on the tile floor. In the mirror, my skin was ashen with bright pink splotches of color on my cheeks. I waited it out, feeling better as my body temperature cooled down.

I toweled off, grabbed a pair of old jeans and followed the smell of bacon and hot coffee.

Shep had tossed off his Stetson, boots, tie and his dress shirt and was standing barefoot in his dark jeans and white t-shirt, folding over a huge omelet in a skillet. His biceps bulged and the fabric strained so much that I swore I could hear it screaming for mercy.

I wanted to trace the ropes of muscle under his skin with my tongue, tasting the combination of sweat and soap and the flavor of Shep. I remembered the heat of him, the solidity of him pressed against me. I didn't know what I was most hungry for at the moment: food or him.

He switched off the burner and turned, stopping dead when he saw me.

I knew the look he had aimed in my direction

He wasn't the first man to want me but he was the first in a long time who got me hard with just the sharp intake of breath that caught deep in his throat.

"Jesus, you're beautiful," he whispered.

I blushed. I hadn't done that in years but his open admiration, genuine wanting made my blood run hot.

Shep's eyes traveled lower, eating up every inch of my naked skin with his hungry gaze. I held my breath until my chest ached with the effort, exhaling slowly as he closed the distance between us. I closed my eyes at the grazing of his fingers down the side of my body and I knew without looking what he was tracing: a black koi fighting against the swirl of the current to travel up and up.

I opened my eyes and saw the question in his eyes.

"It symbolizes the struggle I have everyday." I pointed at my temple. "All the stuff in my head. It's a battle sometimes."

He nodded, his gaze returning to my body. His palm

circled my waist as he walked around me. When he stopped, I was used to his touch and only a deep shiver of pleasure coursed through me when he followed the lines inked there.

"Cherry blossoms. For my mother. They symbolize a life cut short," I explained.

"This is how old?" I squirmed a little when he ghosted a fingertip over a ticklish spot. "You didn't get this recently."

I shook my head, revealing the reason behind this ink. "I got it when she went to prison. She really died when she went in there. Visiting her was like hanging out on the set of 'The Walking Dead'."

His hand traveled up my back and settled with a comforting heavy pressure against the back of my neck. Shep leaned in close and the press of his warm mouth against my shoulder made my insides melt a little bit.

"I'm sorry," he murmured.

I relaxed back into him, accepting what he offered. It felt good to be touched for the sole purpose of comfort without worrying about what Shep wanted in return. Or maybe I just didn't resent that he might want something from me? Or maybe *just* me? Oh hell, this all confused me. Lack of sleep. Stress of the last few months.

He was a mind reader in addition to being a good cook. With a squeeze on my neck, he urged me into one of the chairs at the table.

"You need to eat." He cut the omelet in half and placed each section on a plate, bringing them both to the table. One landed in front of me and the other in the space next to me. He returned with silverware and hot sauce. "Man cannot live by bong alone."

I swiveled my head to the coffee table in front of the fire-place. On it sat my laptop and the bong I'd used a couple of nights ago. I rose to get up and move it out of sight but he placed a hand on my shoulder and pressed me back into my chair.

"Sit, I'll give you a free pass tonight. You've had a rough one," he said with a slight smile that he quickly ruined with a pointed finger. "But put it away the next time I'm coming over. There's only so much I can ignore that's sitting right in front of me."

"So, you think you're coming over again?" I teased, cutting off a piece of the omelet and popping it in my mouth. I groaned. I don't know if I was hungry or if it was the best damn omelet I ever tasted. He was watching me, his eyebrow raised in a knowing tilt. "Okay fine, you can come over again if you promise to cook."

"I have other talents too, you know," he said, throwing a sultry grin at me across the table. I let it go with a grin, concentrating on eating the meal he'd prepared, enjoying the normalcy of the moment after a night of such crazy twists and turns. After several long moments, his next comment surprised me. "*You* have talent, Eli. I looked up your art on your website and it'sstunning."

I blushed, taken off guard with the sincerity of his words. He didn't wait for me to answer.

"It's raw and fierce and I've never seen anything like it." He stood up, gathering our plates and taking them to the sink. "I have no idea where that kind of stuff comes from. I couldn't do it."

I knew where it came from. The dark, twisted bits of myself that were never going to be normal. It had to create things with my hands or lock myself up. That was the choice. My art kept me sane.

"I'd like to sculpt you," I blurted out before I could stop it, no idea how he would take the idea. "In steel. Blue steel. It would match your eyes."

"You could find someone better to sculpt than me."

I stood. Taking the few steps necessary to stand in front of him.

"I would bend the metal to follow the line of your body," I reached out, tracing the line of his bicep, the defined muscle. "Use hammers and mallets to create the texture of your skin, the beat of your heart." I moved down his forearm and the ropy veins underneath the tan of his skin. "Only the strongest of metals to show what kind of man you are." Lifting my hand to follow the line of his jaw and the arch of his brow. I dropped my hand and looked him straight on. "That's why I want to sculpt you, Shepherd Lockwood."

He moved in closer and I saw the rapid rise and fall of his chest under t-shirt. He swept his gaze over me from top to bottom and I knew that the bulge of arousal he saw in my jeans matched the one in his own. I raised my hand again and grabbed the front of his shirt, dragging him close to me. He moaned deep in his throat and I swallowed hard with my own reaction.

Shep leaned in and I lifted my head, allowing him access to my throat. The soft, warm wet press of his tongue and the sharp nips of his teeth went straight to my cock and I arched up on my toes and into his body. My fingers scrambled to get purchase on his t-shirt and I settled on grabbing his ass through his jeans.

His large hands cupped each side of my neck, holding me in place to deliver a deep, thorough kiss. It was hot and wet and filled with aching need. His hands shook and so did mine, the rapid rise of our lust making us awkward and out of sync. We broke apart and he bit at my neck, making me shiver.

I tugged his t-shirt up, grabbing the hem with my fingers and pulling it up his chest. I let him take over the removal of it while I took my chance to run my hands over his skin, the hard muscles of his stomach and the crinkly texture of the dark hair on his chest. I leaned forward and closed my mouth around his nipples, suckling and biting them until he writhed against me.

Shep undid my jeans, shoving them down to mid-thigh and wrapping his fingers around my dick distracting me with his firm, sure strokes. I stumbled backwards, leaning against the countertop, watching as he dropped to his knees at my feet.

His mouth was hot on the skin of my belly, trailing down the faint line of dark hair to the thicker nest at the base of my cock. Shep glanced up at me for the briefest moment and then he lowered his head and sucked me into his mouth.

"Fuck, Shep," I ground out between teeth clenched against the unbelievable pleasure.

His mouth was hot and wet and so very fucking sweet. He sucked me down, using lips and tongue to caress me from root to tip. I reached down and tipped his face up to me and almost lost my stability. His lips were swollen, surrounding my cock, my length wet and slick as he pulled back only to plunge back down again.

I thrust my hips forward and he let me hold his head in place, opening wider on a groan of pleasure. I fucked into his mouth, my fingers wrapped in his dark hair, steel grey eyes locked on mine.

Fire built low in my belly, my orgasm within reach but I didn't want to come that way. No, I wanted more from him. I pulled out of his mouth and grabbed his shoulder, urging him to his feet.

Shep surged up on his feet, his large hands cupping my face as he pulled me into a sex-flavored kiss. His tongue swept along my lower lip, dipping inside before he broke it off, whispering hotly against my mouth, "I want to fuck you, Eli."

"Yes," I readily agreed, unfastening his belt and jeans, dragging him over to the sofa with me. We separated only long enough to kick jeans and boxer briefs to the ground. I paused, drinking my fill of his large, muscled body, lean thighs, thick cock standing taut against his belly. He was stunning.

"I don't know if I could get you right," referring back to our prior conversation.

"Who says I would pose for you?" he teased with a wicked smile.

"Like I'm ever going to forget what you look like."

He leaned in closer, pressing a hot kiss to my collarbone and working his way up my neck to ask, "Lube and a condom?"

I paused. Shit. "I don't have a condom. Only lube."

"I have one," I watched as he walked over to his overnight bag and reached inside, pulling out a toiletry bag. It zipped open and he pulled out a string of foil packets and a small tube.

"I have lube here," I reminded him and pointed to the coffee table next to my laptop.

He stalked over to me, throwing his supplies on the couch, placing his hand on my hips, fingers tracing the line of my muscles that led to my dick. Shep nuzzled under my jawline, falling back on the couch and pulling me down to straddle his hips. "Why do you have lube out here?"

"Because this is where I watch porn."

He laughed. "Naturally."

Shep leaned over and grabbed his bottle, the top clicking open. Slick fingers slid between my cheeks, two pressing into me at once and pushing out a pleading, gasping sound. I gave it over to him, enjoying the burn and the pleasure, loving the stretch. I bore down on his fingers, my fingers digging in.

"Next time I want you to fuck me while we watch your favorite scene," he growled, his lips grazing my own, the sweep of his tongue. "I want to know what you like."

He stretched his fingers inside me, delving in deeper and

teasing my prostate. I pushed against his hand, moaning deeply. "I like this. So much."

Shep teased my lips with his own as he did the same with his fingers in my hole. The pleasure was building again inside of me and I did nothing to hold back the sounds I made. Gasps, pleas, sounds I might be embarrassed about in the morning if Shep was not the man I thought he was.

I reached to my right and snagged the line of condoms, ripping one off and then tearing it open with my teeth. I almost regretted handing it over to him when his fingers slowly slid from inside me but his kiss was soothing, tempting on my lips.

"I want to go slow," he said as he slid the rubber over his length. "But you do it for me. I don't know what it is about you Eli but you make me absolutely, fucking crazy."

I shifted on his lap and reached behind me, guiding his dick until it pressed against my hole. I let him go then, putting my hands on his chest and leaning close as he grasped my cheeks is his large, calloused hands and spread me wide.

"Push back," he ordered and this time I did as I was told. His head entered me, my body resisting for a few, long, tight seconds but I wanted him too much to deny either of us for very long. Shep kissed along my jaw, his fingers now stroking over my sides as he coaxed the last of my fight out me.

I gave in and he slid past the last barrier and I arched back on his dick, loving the sensation of his hot, thick cock deep inside me. Almost immediately he pulled out and then thrust back in, harder and deeper this time. I clenched around him, my muscles tight but the lube assisting the glide.

I reached behind me, my fingers tracing the stretch of my body, the exit and re-entry of his dick and he groaned, low and deep. He gripped my hips, fingers digging deep into the muscle and I knew I'd have bruises there in a day, evidence of just how far I could push Shep Lockwood out of his usual control.

I loved it. I loved bottoming. The surrender and the power of it. The struggle of accommodation and resistance. Opening my body to Shep wasn't difficult at all, everything he was made me want and I was okay with giving into pheromones, attraction, and desire. But I knew that if I stayed here for any amount of time and if I let this man be a part of it, I would have to open something more to him. He would demand it as he had entrance to my body and I didn't know if that was a good or bad thing.

Trouble. The best kind was a little bit of both.

Grabbing his shoulders once again, I looked down at him as I added my own rise and fall to our rhythm, meeting his upward thrust until I feel his hips against my ass, his thighs pressed tightly against mine. My cock slapped and rubbed against the hard planes of his stomach with every circuit but the friction wasn't enough. I needed more. It was like he could read my mind.

"Jack yourself off, I want to see it," Shep demanded, a wicked tease on his lips. "I'll fuck you hard as long as I see your cock in your hand. Do it."

I didn't want him to stop what he was doing, the girth of him stretched me so good and he was rubbing against my prostate with every pass so I did it. I wrapped my fingers around my dick and I stroked myself from root to tip. It was amazing, Shep inside me and my own touch on the outside. I could feel the rise of pleasure deep in my belly but I didn't fight it this time. I just let it build and build.

"Fuck, Eli." Shep ground out between clenched teeth, his face and chest slick with his sweat. "So goddam gorgeous. You feel so good, tight."

He pounded into me from below and I sped up my own stroking as I felt the first pulse of my orgasm in my balls. My body clenched around him and his loud breathing hitched as I felt his hand push aside my own to take hold of my dick.

His touch was rougher, less knowing but the total surrender of my pleasure to him was like a thousand jolts of electricity to my body. I gave him the control, concentrating on riding him, my head thrown back.

"Ride my cock. Come all over me," his voice was roughened to gravel and I gave into his obvious desire and my unbearable need and I gave him my release. I came in hot, ropy spurts all over his chest, my shout unchecked and consisting of nothing more than his name over and over.

Shep sped up his thrusts, pushing in even deeper for a few seconds longer and then he was coming too, his large body taut underneath me. He was frozen for a moment, almost as if I'd been able to sculpt him in that second and I soaked in the sight, filing it away for later. To capture that moment of his ecstasy in any form would be something to work for, something to keep me up for many days and nights.

I collapsed against him, not caring that my come was cooling between us and would stick us together like glue eventually. There are worse ways to end up.

He was still buried inside me and I sighed when he made a move to separate us.

"I know," he agreed, "I'd like to stay too."

He slid out and I eased off him, flopping down on the couch on my side, watching as he disposed of the condom. When he eased down next to me, his legs and arms tangling with mine to make room for two grown men on the width of the sofa, I was happy to have him there, skin-to-skin, again.

Shep leaned over and kissed me, soft and deep. It was sweet in comparison to what we'd just done and I liked that he could be both. The softness in his grey eyes hit me right in the chest and I groaned, wanting to scramble away and drag him even closer at the same time. It only scared me because I knew he could see the same thing in my own.

The sex was good, amazing but the connection that we had

was dangerous. It wasn't love, not even close, but I could see myself getting to the point where I'd want to keep him.

"Yeah, I know," he said and I really began to wonder if he could read my mind. "It's like I said, Eli. Trouble. Nothing but trouble."

"But are we the good kind or the bad kind?"

He stared at me and I didn't flinch away. The seconds stretched into a long moments before he spoke. "I think we'll just have to wait and see."

Chapter Nine

Ah. Home sweet home.

I gazed around the large entryway of the Sutherland Mansion. Nothing had changed in the eight years since I'd gone away. Same cold marble floor. Same pretentious "look at me" staircase. Same portraits of perpetually constipated Sutherland ancestors.

I was never so grateful to look like my mother as when I stood in this room.

The light steps of one of the many staff approached from my left and I turned.

"Mr. Sutherland will see you in his study."

I nodded and followed her down the long corridor. The large double doors were closed but she knocked briskly and when Bud's rumbling "come in" traveled out to us, I grabbed the handle and moved inside the room, closing it behind me.

Bud was sitting behind his huge desk, a cigar in his hand as he rifled through an avalanche of papers. He glanced up at me and roughly motioned for me to come in.

"I won't embarrass either one of us by pretending this is a social call. I presume you're here to talk about ranch business and my first question is how much you want for it," he barked out.

I didn't particularly like the old man but I did appreciate his style.

"I'm not interested in selling Shadow Ranch."

That got his attention and he stopped his paper shuffling and glared at me across the desktop.

"Are going to stay then? Because you don't know shit about running a ranch of that size."

I laughed. He wasn't wrong. "I don't but I find myself short a ranch manager at the moment and I wanted to borrow one of yours for the short time I need to find a replacement. Now."

And I wasn't exaggerating. I'd spent the better part of a day and a half trying to make sense of his ledgers and account. I only knew enough about cattle and feed and nutrition cycles to be dangerous. Admitting defeat at this point was a relief.

He stared at me, obviously rolling something around his in his head. Probably trying to calculate just how much it will cost to get rid of me once and for all. Good luck. I didn't want any of his money. My determination must have been all over my face because, to my surprise, he didn't waste any time fighting me.

"I've got a man who's ready to take over his own operation. Young. Has a pretty little wife and a son. He's a hard worker and I figure I've got him for another year at the most in his current position. You can try him on for size and if he works, hire him."

I blinked. I expected a fight or at least a long, drawn-out negotiation. This offer wassuspicious.

"What will this cost me? What will I owe you?" I asked. Better to know than to wonder.

He laughed, big and booming and I jumped in the chair. Holy shit. I could count on one hand the number of times the old man didn't try to cut me dead with his glare. The fit he was having right now made me wonder if I should call a doctor.

"Nothing. You won't owe me a thing," he said, pointing at me across the desk as his laughter died away. "But this makes us even. I feel like I owe you a debt, boy. The Sutherlands always pay their debts."

Okay, now this was just freakish. Maybe I was still at home, having weird dreams in a pot-induced haze? Stranger things had happened.

"Alright. I'll bite. What do you think you owe me?"

"WeI knew what was going on at your house and I did nothing. I wasn't going to get in the middle of my brother's business but I think I should have. If I had maybe"

He didn't need to finish the sentence. We both knew what might have been different if they'd all taken a stand instead of ignoring what was right in front of their noses.

How many nights and days had I raged against the world, against myself and played the "what if" game? Too many. Way too fucking many.

"You were wrong. You should have helped my mother, me," I said, my voice surprisingly even and steady.

"Yes."

We stared at each other across the room and juggled the way this would go.

"What is this? A truce?" I asked.

He shrugged. "We can bury the proverbial hatchet on the fence line between our ranches."

"As long as it's not in my back."

"Jesus, you always were such an overly dramatic boy."

I stood. "It's the artistic temperament."

He let that go. "So you're not selling but are you staying?"

I thought back to last night. Gray eyes. Big hands. Open smile.

"For a little while."

Chapter Ten

I was still amazed at how dark it was on the ranch at night.

Years of living in the city of Austin and the near-constant level of lighting had me squinting and blinking to try to relieve a little bit of the utter blackness just beyond the reach of the headlights. Stars over head and solar powered lights lining the long driveway barely made a dent in the dark and the lights in the main house were like a mirage in the distance.

I glanced down at my phone when the screen came to life. Shep. I tapped the "answer" button and his voice filled the cab of my truck. I smiled at the low rumble.

"What are you doing?"

"Just driving back from meeting with Bud."

"And I didn't get an emergency call to come identify the dead body?"

I laughed. "Believe or not, we decided to bury the hatchet."

"In whose back?" Excellent question.

"Neither, for now," I said, the truck rocking as it hit a deep divot in the driveway. "What are you doing tonight?"

"I thought you might *do* me," he said, smooth as glass. I grinned.

Shep Lockwood was worth staying around to figure out. At least until he couldn't surprise me anymore.

"Dirty. Dirty. It's so shocking to hear that come out of your mouth. Officer Lockwood, you're usually soreserved," I teased.

"Still waters and all that," he said, pausing only briefly before continuing. "Wait and see how dirty I get when you're fucking me."

I shifted in my seat, my cock getting hard enough to make my jeans just a little too tight. "Well then, I'll leave the light on for you."

"I'll be there soon."

I ended the call and drove the last few hundred feet to the front of the house. I pulled the truck into the spot I now thought of as "mine" and shut off the engine. Sliding out of the cab I shut the door and headed for the steps when I heard a noise coming from the direction of the barns.

I stopped, straining my ears. Nothing.

I turned to walk back into the house.

And thenI heard it again.

A scrape. A heavy tool being used. Voices.

I descended the steps and proceeded as quietly as I could across the driveway, flinching with every crunch of the pea gravel. I made a mental note to see how much it would cost to pave whole damn thing.

The sounds grew louder as I got closer to the cluster of buildings. I moved into the shadows of the first barn, the snuffling sounds of the horses inside the building temporarily masking the scrapes of metal againstwhat the hell was that noise? I skated around the edge of the barn and the noises got louder, the voices more urgent.

I peered around the corner and immediately saw the truck pulled up in front of the third barn. Two men were inside, their figures silhouettes against the light cast by a lantern placed in the middle of the entrance.

I moved in closer to get a better look, making the effort to stay in the shadows and out of their line of sight. I wasn't dumb enough to take on two men who were obviously doing something they didn't want to be seen. I pulled my phone out of my pocket and hit Shep's number in the list of recent calls. He answered on the second ring.

"I can't use the emergency lights to get there any sooner, Eli," he said, his voice tinged with warmth and laughter. "That could get me fired."

"There are two men here," I hissed into the phone. I felt ridiculous but I couldn't risk being overheard.

"Look, I know we don't know each other all that well yet but I'm not a fan of orgies. At least not on a night where I have to go to work tomorrow."

I rolled my eyes and then felt stupid because he couldn't see me. "No. There are two men stealing from my barn. Right now."

A long moment passed and I could actually feel him slip into cop mode. When he spoke his voice dipped lower on a growl.

"What? Where are you?"

"I'm watching them from the adjacent building. I can't see what they're taking."

"Jesus. Eli, don't go in there." When I didn't answer him right away he insisted. "I'm serious, Eli. Don't you fucking go in there. These guys have already bashed you over the head and killed Kevin Fry."

"Well, then hurry up and get here and be the cavalry," I ducked farther back into the shadows when one of them emerged from the barn door and hoisted something into the bed of the truck. "They're putting something in the back of a truck. I can't see what it is."

"Don't move. I don't like it when you get hurt, Eli," he growled and the combination of his words and his tone made me shiver. Yeah, I could get used to Shep Lockwood and his particular Texas Alpha brand of sexy. "I'll call it in and get backup there as well."

He ended the call and I put my full attention back on the illegal activity happening in my barn.

The men had gone back into the building, disappearing into the left side where the large Caterpillar was parked. I could hear the sound of whatever tool they were using scraping and banging against metal. They were far enough away from the entrance that I couldn't see who they were or what they were doing from my current position.

I crouched lower and slid along the side of the building, getting as close as I could to the entrance. I concentrated, straining to hear anything over the noise.

"Be careful. Don't cut into it."

"Just one more."

"Fucking Kevineasier with the keys."

"Last one."

Damn. They were almost done with whatever they were doing. I didn't know how long it would take Eli to get here but I didn't want them to get away without getting a look at them or stopping them from leaving. I looked over my shoulder at their truck, gauging the distance and the shadows and wondered how long it would take me to disable it.

These people had killed Kevin and tried to kill me. I wasn't up to hand-to-hand combat but I definitely could take the central wire on the distributor cap

I crouched low to the ground and ran as fast as I could across the open yard, sliding along the side of the truck opposite of the lantern. It wasn't as dark here but it was better than nothing and I could still see the open doors while popping the hood.

Easing the door open, I peered into the truck cab and spied the keys dangling from the ignition. Fuck yeah. I leaned across the seat and grabbed the bundle of keys, slipping them into my pocket and easing back out of the truck cab. I quietly shut the door and intended to slip back into the shadows without being seen.

I was out of luck.

I turned and almost ran into a stranger. Large, burly and very surprised. He recovered quickly.

"Larkin, get out here. Quick," he shouted, not taking his eyes off me or moving out of the way. I cut my eyes to the left, gauging whether I could out run him. "Don't even think about it."

He pulled a gun out of his jacket and aimed it at me. I took a step back, as if that would make all the difference if he decided to fire it and try to take my head off. Standing still was my best option at this point. Hopefully I could keep them talking long enough for Shep to get here with his weapon and backup.

"Larkin!"

"What the fuck do you want?" The second man came out of the barn and rounded the back of the truck, stopping suddenly when he spied me. I took a long look at him, his face also unrecognizable. I had no idea who these two men were but they knew me.

"That's Eli Sutherland. That faggot bastard who owns this place." He moved even closer pointing at me. "What the fuck is he doing here?"

The first man shook his head but the gun didn't waiver. "Don't know. I just came out and he was standing here."

Larkin, the second man, approached me. He reached out with a large hand and grabbed my arm, giving me a shake that rammed my bruised side into the truck. I winced and he shoved me again, this time a bit a harder. I bit back any reaction this time, unwilling to give him the satisfaction.

"What the fuck were you doing out here Sutherland?"

"You're not as quiet as you think you are," I spit out, trying to wrench my arm away. He only gripped me tighter and since he had about fifty pounds on me, there wasn't much I could do if I couldn't catch him off guard. "I came down here to see what you were stealing." I strained towards the back of the truck. "What's in there? Drugs?"

Bingo. They both flinched and I knew I'd hit on the answer.

"Shut the fuck up." This time is was the guy with the gun. I tried to swerve as much as I could as he waved the gun around and prayed he still had the safety on. Larkin's hand loosened on my arm when he focused on his partner. A perfect opportunity for me to make a break for it, if I could get them, and keep them, agitated. It was a planalmost.

I decided to go for broke and ask all the questions.

"Which one of you shot Kevin Fry?" I looked at the guy holding the gun. "I'm guessing it was you." I nodded at Larkin. "This guy doesn't seem like he's got the guts to shoot somebody."

I had no basis for my trash talk but it didn't matter, Larkin's ego made him sloppy.

"What the fuck? I fucking shot that dick. He was getting cold feet, afraid you'd find out and fire him." He shook me for emphasis, my back jamming into the side view mirror. I sucked in my hiss of pain. I didn't know if Larkin had actually shot Kevin but he sure as hell knew how to make sure I bounced every bruised part of my body on the hardest parts of the truck. "I got sick of his whining so I shot his ass. We owe this stuff to people who only understand on time shipments and money and I ain't dying because Kevin was a pussy."

Larkin didn't sound like he minded at all that he'd blown a guy away that he'd known so I didn't assume that he'd have any trouble killing me.

I looked over my shoulder, straining to see headlights or

hear sirens. Where the hell was Shep? Where the hell was anybody with a badge and a service weapon?

A shadow moving on the far edge of the opposite side of the barn caught my eye. I knew that shape, would know it anywhere even in the dark. I sagged a little bit in relief and then braced myself to cause some chaos to give Shep a time to do his thing.

Larkin had other plans.

"Murray, shoot him. He's a problem we don't need."

Larkin raised the gun a little higher and I started babbling. "I don't know anything"

I could see that he didn't care by the cold blankness in his eyes. Wherever you had to go to kill someone in cold blood, Murray had purchased the ticket and was already gone. I shut my eyes when he aimed the pistol right at my head.

The shot made me jump but I didn't feel the impact and I hoped to God that Shep had been the one who fired. I opened my eyes in time to see Murray clutch his shoulder, the gun dangled limply in his hand but he didn't drop it. I jammed my elbow into Larkin's side and while I knew it wouldn't take him down, I took the chance to wrench out of his grasp and run for the barn.

Larkin yelled and followed close on my heels, hands grabbing my shirt, my jeans. I heard a rip but I kept going, hoping to be able to put something solid between me and this lunatic. I had no weapon and I knew he could kill me before Shep could get to me.

Shots rang out over my head and wood splintered in the doorframe next to me as I bolted inside. Larkin had recovered enough to fire off a few rounds I guessed but I had to leave him to Shep.

I skidded across the floor and grabbed the first thing in my view, my propane blowtorch. Flipping off the safety valve and turning on the flow was like second nature and I aimed it at

Larkin. His momentum was too fast for him to stop and dodge so the flame hit him on the neck and shoulder. The smell of burning fabric, skin and hair coated my nostrils as his screams filled my ears.

He fell back, writhing on the ground as the figures of several Sheriff's deputies were framed by the open doors. Murray stood still, the gun dropping to the ground as he raised his hands in the air. I sucked in as much air as I could, trying hard to comprehend what was happening in all of the chaos.

Shep rounded the corner, gun drawn as he searched the space. When our eyes locked, he relaxed a little and slid his gun into his shoulder holster. He approached me slowly, his gaze flickering to the lit torch and over to where Larkin was being detained by two officers.

"You want to turn that off, Eli?" He asked, nodding to the flaming torch hissing in my hand.

I stared at him for a few moments, his words taking time to register in my brain with all the other crap taking space in there. I nodded, found the off switch and tossed the torch on the nearby bench, using the same piece of furniture to lean against.

Shep was there, his warm hands on my face, hard body pressed against me. "Are you okay?"

He felt good. Really good.

I nodded, taking a moment to swallow before answering him, "I'm not shot. Or dead" I leveled a worried glance at him. "Aren't you pissed? You told me to stay away from them."

"I'll be pissed later," he said, his voice holding enough of a growl to know that I would be getting my ass chewed later. And then he leaned in and kissed me. A short exchange of breath and soft lips to assure each other that we would live to fight later.

When he pulled back, the swarm of bodies behind him grew with the flashing of red and blue lights and uniformed personnel. Two paramedics headed in my direction and I groaned, prompting Shep to glance over his shoulder.

"Just once, I'd like for the time I see you to not involve interrogation rooms or medical equipment," I grumbled, hanging onto him a little tighter as the adrenaline wore off. I hurt. All over.

He hung onto me, laughing softly. "I think I can deliver if you're staying around for a while."

"I'm staying. For a while."

He returned my steady gaze. "Good."

Shep pressed a brief kiss before the paramedics descended on me, the murmur against my ear meant only for me. "Trouble. Nothing but trouble." Another soft kiss against my temple. "Only the good kind."

Epilogue

A month later

"Don't peek."

I led Shep into the best position to see the piece, careful to not let him trip over the uneven floor of the barn. I'd finished my original piece and then started on this one, working steadily, day and night to get it right.

It had taken time, finding the right way to temper the metal to the blue hue I wanted and then forming it into the shape that had jumped into my mind fully formed. My refusal to let him see the progress had been a source of much teasing and bickering. I'd loved it and I think he did too.

Now my stomach did a tumble. I hoped he liked it.

I'd seen a lot of Shep Lockwood in the past month. We saw each other three or four days a week when his work permitted. Some of his things were hanging in my closet or in a drawer I'd offered up after week two. We had even gone one weekend to Austin to pick up more of my things. I still wasn't ready to sell or leave the city entirely and I struggled to find a way to keep both ends going.

I didn't have any answers yet and he wasn't pushing. We were enjoying each other. Learning about each other. There was no rush. We had time to get it right.

"Okay, are you ready?" I asked, laughing when he growled out his frustration.

"I've been ready for a month. Stop being a dick and let me see it."

"Okay." I took a deep breath. "Look."

He opened his eyes and looked. I still had a hard time reading him when he wanted to conceal something from me. His cop face was blank and it drove me nuts that he could give nothing away while his brain was whirring like a hamster on a wheel behind the scenes.

Now was one of those times and I moved back and waited.

The piece was huge. Almost as tall as the two of us, it rose in a column of twists and turns toward the sky. The metal was thick as it formed the loose shapes that merged together and appeared to move as you moved around it.

"I see a dragon," he said, walking around the back of it. He soaked in every detail, gaze moving from place to place. "A man as well. It looks like they are one thing. Meshed into one being."

I nodded, unable to keep the grin off my face. He saw what it was but from the hint of confusion in his voice, he didn't understand.

"The Japanese dragon is symbol of strength and wisdom. Power used to benefit people, to help." He looked at me then, understanding rising like dawn on his face. "I took the shape of your body, your hands, your back and merged it with the dragon. He is in you and you are in him." I pointed to a place where the man and the beast undulated together. "They don't fight each other because they are the same thing."

I stopped talking because he was on me, his hands cupping my face and his mouth on mine. His tongue swept inside, possessing and caressing at the same time, demanding my response. I gave it. There was no reason not to.

There was no pretense with Shep. No games. No manipulation.

He wasn't perfect. He was sloppy and had a short fuse when he was overtired. He nagged me about the pot and didn't really click with my friends from the art scene. He pushed me to try and make nice with my Uncle Bud.

But he also told me what he liked and told me what he didn't. He was honest and tried to lean more about my world. He held me when I had my nightmares and he still made the best damn omelet I'd ever tasted.

He was like a rock. Solid but hard, a support but also rough enough to cause damage when you beat against it.

He broke off the kiss and looked down at me. "That's how you see me?"

I nodded. "Yep. I do."

He swallowed hard, his hands shaking a little bit. "That's the kind of guy you fall for. Stick around long term for."

I nodded again. "Yep. It is."

A pause. The span of a few heartbeats and then he smiled.

It was enough. For now.

FREE AGENT

His future, His career. His Heart. Everything is on the line . . .

Defenseman James "DC" Washington has had a big year: winning "The Cup" and coming out to his team and the entire world were events that changed his life. Now a free agent, he thought he had his next step all planned out . . . until the man he might not be able to resist puts a sexy offer on the table.

For Karin.
You are missed every day.

DC

"Edwin, if you say the words 'the Cup' one more time before we reach Washington, I will beat you with it."

The tall, gangly dude standing next to me on the gangway to the plane opened his mouth and pushed his huge glasses up on his nose as he met me eye-to-eye and toe-to-toe. Edwin Motz was as tall as I was but I was bigger and I used every inch of my professional hockey player body to make my point. "You've lectured me every minute of the last three hours on the proper way to touch 'the Cup', to look at 'the Cup', to think about 'the Cup' or to even refer to 'the Cup'. I'm done. For the two hours of this flight, I'm done."

"Mr. Washington," he protested, his voice perfectly pitched in the usual tone of reverence as he draped his arm protectively around the huge, padlocked container which housed the cup when it traveled with its very nervous caretaker. "If you fail to uphold the standards of dealing with 'the Cup' that falls on my shoulders. I have to ensure that you understand. . ."

I cut him off as an airline representative approached him with an orange bag-check tag and an earnest expression.

"Edwin, *I understand*. It's crystal fucking clear. I'm a professional hockey player and if *anyone* understands the importance of the cup housed inside that absurdly large container, it's me." I hefted my carry-on over my shoulder and moved towards the entrance of the plane where a very pretty flight attendant was waiting with a first-class seat with my name on it. I threw my last warning over my shoulder. "I mean it, Edwin. You're the man and you do a great job but if you talk to me about 'the Cup" before we land in D.C., I will cut you."

At my seat, I grabbed my iPad and earbuds out of my bag before I shoved it into the overhead container and gave the attendant my request for an orange juice. My seat was the one by the window and I eased down into it, wedging my six feet two inch, two hundred pound frame into a seat not quite designed for a guy my size. Still, it was better than coach and I sent up a prayer of thanks to the Cajun Rage's travel office for booking this seat even though I was going to Washington to potentially accept a job with another team. It really wasn't a surprise. The front office was a class act.

I fastened my seat belt and then eased back into the leather cushion, letting out a huge sigh of almost-relief. Either way, I'd know my future at the end of this weekend and it eased some of the tension that had been sitting in between my shoulder blades for the better part of three months, well, ever since I decided to go out as a free agent. Closing my eyes, I let the sounds of the other first-class passengers roll over me as I my mind drifted over day's agenda. It was going to be a long-ass day.

Who was I kidding? It had been a long-ass year. Ever since I'd decided to hold the press conference and tell the world that I was gay, my life had been nothing but a roller coaster. Supportive teammates, asshole teammates, fans who had my back and those who'd held up posters at games telling me that someone with my sexual preference didn't belong on the ice.

I'd spent twelve months finding out who my friends really were and saying good riddance to those who weren't.

A. Long. Ass. Year.

A familiar voice, pissy and gruff, made me open my eyes and look around. I eyeballed Edwin as he walked past me, talking on the phone to someone about my failure to respect "the cup" or some bullshit and I ignored his narrow-eyed glare. He had a tough job but that guy needed to lighten the fuck up. It wasn't like I planned to parachute out of the plane with the thing. It was just going to a youth center full of teenagers who were better behaved than most of my teammates. I was glad when he passed the open seat behind me and took one just behind me next to the window. Cool. I was safe from any more lectures for two hours, at least.

"Hey Jamie, where y'at?"

My body knew exactly who it was before I opened my eyes. The whisky-smooth voice dripping with a deep bayou burr belonged to the hot-as-fuck man who'd kept me panting after him for the three years I'd played for the Rage. I eased my eyes open and soaked in all six feet four inches of man, body taut with muscle, skin the color of a deep mocha and brown eyes edged with gold. This morning his long, natural afro was pulled back into a low ponytail and his smile was wide and sincere framed by a goatee.

If I had a dollar for every time I pictured his lips wrapped around my cock, I'd be able to buy my own professional hockey team.

And I loved the fact that he called me Jamie. Nobody else did that.

"Hey Etienne," I swallowed hard, pushing down the nervous shake in my voice.

I was completely into this guy and although I'd caught the looks he shot in my direction from time-to-time, we'd never taken it anywhere. It wasn't because he hadn't known I was interested. My body had given me away at every opportunity by popping a boner whenever he put his hands on me in PT. He'd ignored it. I'd ignored it. I'd told myself that it was because he was on the medical staff of the team and there was a conflict of interest but I knew it was because I hadn't been out and he'd never been in. In the world of gay men it was like I lived on Mars and he lived on Earth. That was a distance too far to cross.

And here he was, looking at me like I was the prize at the bottom of his Cracker Jack box with a first class boarding pass in his hand. If there was a God, he would have the seat next to me.

As if he heard my thoughts, he tossed his phone on the seat in question and lifted a carry-on bag into the overhead, taking a few moments to rummage around for whatever he needed out of it. I watched him, trying not to let on that I was ogling the strip of skin exposed when he lifted his arms and his t-shirt hiked up with the movement. Dark skin, the glimpse of a six-pack and a treasure trail of black hair leading into the waist-band of his cargo shorts. Holy hell.

I took it back. There was a God after all and he loved me.

He finished what he was doing and picked up his phone and slid into the seat. He pulled a set of earbuds out of his pocket and slid the male end into the female opening before fastening his seat belt. All set, he turned and gave me his biggest smile. My heart rate kicked up a notch. His smile was breathtaking.

I decided that staring and drooling was going to edge into odd and creepy if I didn't say something soon. "You going to DC or is that just a connection?"

"Nope. I'm going to hang out with some friends for the weekend. I love the city and plan to do some cheesy tourist stuff while I'm there." He jerked his thumb over his shoulder and towards where Edwin sat behind me. "Is this your day with 'the cup'?"

"Yep. Taking it to some inner-city kids at a local youth center. I do some work with them and I promised that I would if we won."

"That's cool."

"I hope so. They're good kids."

"So, you going to meet with the DC team like all the rumors are saying?" He asked, startling me with his directness. While we'd all skated around the issue, none of my teammates or the staff had asked me directly what I was going to do now that I was a free agent.

I nodded. "My agent and I have a meeting with the DC team. I'm still not sure what I'm going to do."

He eyed me carefully, breaking the contact when the flight attendant brought my juice and asked for his order. When she was gone he zeroed back in on me, his deep brown eyes narrowed with suspicion.

"That's bullshit. You know what you want to do and what you're going to do." He leaned in close enough for me to get a whiff of his spicy aftershave and the mint gum on his breath. He made a cross-cross motion on his chest and lowered his voice to a seductive level. "I promise I won't go tattling back to the big boss."

I grinned back at him, rolling my eyes at his foolishness. Etienne was always upbeat, teasing and joking with everyone. His easy manner and quick wit made him an excellent PT and his constant flirtation had made him my secret crush. If a grown ass man of my age could have one of those. What the hell. I'd know this weekend what my future held so it wouldn't hurt to let him in.

I locked eyes with him as I moved in closer, our faces close enough for our breath to mingle. My arm brushed his and he shifted towards me, aligning our sides on the arm rest between us as the moment dragged out. When I finally spoke, my voice was ragged edged and rough with the desire for him rushing through my veins. I could see his pulse throbbing on his neck, just under the beard stubbled skin and I longed to lean forward and lick and suck on that spot until he groaned against me.

As if he could read my mind, his eyes dilated with his own desire and I was the one biting back a groan.

"If they offer me a decent deal, I'll take it. DC is my home." I wondered if he could hear the tinge of regret in my words.

He cocked his head, his smile fading a bit at the edges. "Oh Jamie, I was hoping that it was a rumor."

We stared at each other, the sounds of the plane preparing for departure just distant background noise. I focused on him, the way he said my name with that sexy southern drawl and the disappointment coating each word. Once again I regretted not pursuing this thing between us. If DC didn't offer for me, no small consolation would be seeing where this attraction between us would lead back in New Orleans.

I gave in and indulged in a little harmless flirting. I was no player but I could hold my own. And this might be my last chance to do this with Etienne.

"Will you miss me if I go?"

Etienne stared. The only indication that he'd heard was his rushed intake of breath and the wetting of his lips. I leaned in to repeat my question directly in his ear, hoping to coax out a shiver this time, when a figure appeared over his shoulder. Dressed in blue. Perky. Smiling.

Our flight attendant stood there holding Etienne's ginger ale and he pulled away, retreating slightly to the other side of his seat and creating distance between us. I settled back in my own space watching the ground crew prepare the airplane for departure and wishing that the friendly skies had better timing.

Etienne

The flight attendant saved my ass.

Jamie Washington was a bad idea and I knew it. A sexy, shy, bear of a man who flipped every switch I had. Even when I'd been with David there had been a sexual gravity between us, pulling us into each other's orbit. And yeah, I'd noticed how hard he'd gotten every time I put my hands on him. Only the discretion afforded by my own uniform pants had spared us from ending up horizontal on my treatment table and jeopardizing both our jobs. The team didn't prohibit fraternization but getting off when I was supposed to be treating a player would have been too far over the line.

But *this close* on an airplane? So close I could smell his warm scent and the woodsy cologne he preferred? Jesus. I've never been the one to look for trouble but Jamie was a temptation and I'd gladly follow wherever he led. I slurped down half my drink to cool off my libido, leaning back in my seat as the flight crew went over the safety instructions and the plane took off for Washington, DC. I counted the seconds as they crawled by. I couldn't do this for the next two hours.

But small talk? I sucked at it.

"So, you're visiting friends? Any special occasion?" Shy Jamie broke the silence and I relaxed with gratitude. I was normally an outgoing guy. Born and bred in New Orleans I was the poster child for *Laissez le bon temps rouler.* But with this quiet man with the smoky gray eyes? I was tongue-tied more often than not.

I shrugged. "Nothing special. I haven't been there in a while and it won't be long before the season cranks up and the only travel I'll be doing is with the team. I'm going to play the tourist, make the *veiller* with my friends."

"You got a place to stay? The agent booked me at this cool hotel in Dupont Circle."

"I'm staying with my buddy Ryker. His place is near there. I love that area of town. People are always around and the bars and restaurants are all so cool."

"Ryker?" Jamie asked, his nose scrunching up in confusion as his smile shown out from the middle of his dark beard. "One name? Like Madonna? Bono? RuPaul?"

I let loose the laugh that bubbled up at that comment. "He's more like 'Sons of Anarchy' but I'll make sure to tell him that you compared him to a drag queen. That'll go over really well."

Jamie held up his hands in surrender. "Hey man, I'm not looking for any trouble. Not this close to the season starting. What do you want to do? End my career before it takes off?"

"I'd say that winning the championship the season you come out as the first openly gay player in the league pretty much says that your career has taken off. You've got liftoff. You're orbiting the universe right now."

"Let's just hope that I can stay up there." Jamie lapsed into silence, his gaze drifting towards the window and the blue skies and fluffy clouds passing us by. His hands clenched and unclenched in his lap, his right leg bouncing up and down and betraying his obvious anxiety at the decisions before him. He was a patient who fidgeted on the table but this was different. He had so many decisions to make, I totally understood.

And after the year he'd had, he was handling it all really well.

"I was proud when you came out man," I said before I realized the words were leaving my brain and shooting out my mouth. He swiveled towards me, both the smile and confusion back on his face.

"I appreciate that but you already told me." He reached out and touched arm, giving it a light squeeze before pulling it back again in a lingering stroke. "You even showed up at the press conference. That was . . . really amazing. You have no idea how much that meant to me to see someone like you there, having my back."

"Someone like me?"

"Yeah." He dipped his head down but not enough where I missed the blush of embarrassment across his cheeks. "Men who were out and proud. Men who had the guts to be who they were. I can only imagine what you thought of me."

I shook my head, really not understanding this at all. "What I thought of you? Jamie, I admit that I wasn't thrilled when I figured out you were in the closet but that wasn't because I looked down on you."

"Come on. You don't have to say that." He pushed back, his head shaking in denial at my words. "I was a coward."

"Fuck that. You were a guy in a game where *nobody* was out. *Nobody*. And you had no idea if being yourself would take you away from a game you loved. I got it. I still get it but I was fucking pissed that you had to make that choice." I looked down and realized that I had the front of his t-shirt gripped in my hand and I was pulling him closer as the conversation heated. Our faces were inches apart once more and it took everything in me not to close the distance and see what he tasted like once and for all. "But I was never pissed at you,

Jamie. Never. What you did took guts and balls the size of Texas. I went to the press conference because I wasn't sure if I'd ever see anyone be that brave again in my lifetime."

He stared at me, his gaze flickering between my eyes and my mouth and I knew that one shift towards him by me and he'd kiss me. Fuck but I wanted to know. But this was stupid. I had no business starting something I knew would end when he got the offer from the enemy team. And no matter how fun I'd had hooking up since David had moved out, I was looking for something more now.

I let go of his shirt and lightly pushed at his chest, sending him back into his seat as I settled back into mine.

"Well, I'm not the hero you make me out to be but that means a lot. Coming from you . . ." he paused, gathering his thoughts. ". . . from you that really means something."

My "rah-rah" speech ended the conversation again but this time it wasn't awkward. We both retreated for a bit, settling into the flight and ordering another round of drinks. I didn't want to grill him the entire thousand mile flight but there was something I really wanted to know. I wasn't sure if he'd tell me but that never stopped me before.

"You didn't have to do it, Jamie. I'm just wondering *why* you decided to come out."

Jamie had been thumbing through his playlist on his phone but he stopped his action and looked at me. This time the smile teasing at his lips wasn't seductive. It was . . .playful. Like he had a delicious secret and he wasn't sure if he was going to share it or not. And just when I thought he'd refuse to tell me, he responded with a question.

"What are you doing this afternoon?"

"Nothing."

"Come with me and I'll show you."

And that was a deal I couldn't pass up.

DC

_____

I heard them before I saw them. As always, they made me smile.

A wall of sound preceded the group of twenty teenagers pouring into the large recreational space of the Anacostia Youth Center. Etienne took a step back in surprise at the noise, moving further to my right when they bypassed the large, towering silver goblet and headed straight for me.

I braced myself for impact, my arms extended to return hugs or high-fives to the kids I'd begun to think of as my own younger brothers and sisters. They were even louder up close and I spied Edwin inching closer to the cup, his arms flexing protectively as the kids kicked their excitement up a notch or twelve.

"DC!"

"Yo man. You gettin' huge."

"You gonna come play for a real team soon?"

I laughed as they talked over each other, the trash talk growing as they tried to out do each other. These kids - all LGBTQ - had become a family for each other in the two years the program had officially begun, gaining pride and strength with each day spent together. I was proud to be a member of the Rage but these kids . . . they were the real champions in my mind.

"Hey!" I shouted over the noise, letting out a loud wolf whistle that cut through their crap and brought the room down a relative level of silence. I pointed at Etienne and he waved to all of them, his smile warm but a little shy. "This is my friend, Etienne. He's on the medical staff of the Rage."

"Is he your boyfriend DC?" J.J. asked, his eyebrows wagging up and down in a move that was supposed to be dirty but only came out as comical since he couldn't make them shift up and down at the same time. He looked more like a clown with weird party tricks than a teenager trying to embarrass me with a suggestive leer about my sex life. I looked at Etienne and found him eyes wide, biting back a laugh. He was going to be no help so I turned back to the mob.

"No. He's a friend and you need to be nice."

J.J. threw his hands up in a gesture of "whatever" but I ignored him. His teasing was harmless. A sign that he was comfortable with me and not one of disrespect.

"Remember how I told you guys that I'd bring the cup back with me if we won?"

"You also said you'd buy us pizza and soda," Tyrique reminded me as he rubbed his belly. At over six feet tall and on the upper end of one-hundred-ninety pounds, I knew he cared more about the food than the cup.

"I did and I'm here to keep that promise." I pointed towards the cup and the man charged with keeping it safe. "That is Mr. Motz and you do exactly what he says when it comes to the cup. You can have your picture taken with it, with me. Anything goes as long as you're respectful and careful. If I have to buy a new one because you knuckleheads broke it, I'll bust some heads. I promise you that."

They all stared at me, eyes huge and full of surprise for one hot minute and then they burst out into laughter. Blowing off my threats they rolled their eyes and headed to the cup and an anxious Edwin. He held his own though, handling the kids with stern direction. They lined up, mugging for the camera as the photographer snapped pictures as fast as they could switch poses.

I snagged Tyrique by the back of his collar before he could head over to hog the camera. "Did I even scare them a little bit?"

He shook his head, his smile shy but open. He was a gentle giant and I could count on him to keep the other kids in line. He had a gift with children and I couldn't wait to see what he did with it.

"No way, DC," he said. "You don't have to threaten them. They're more afraid of disappointing you than getting a beat down. They'll keep it straight for you, man. You don't have to worry about that."

He bolted to join the group and I found myself smiling.

"That says a lot about you, Jamie." Etienne observed, his shoulder brushing mine as he moved in closer. I got a whiff of his aftershave, a complicated scent that was made up of spice and fire and summer nights. It made my mouth water and I steadied my breath under the intense weight of his gaze. "You've really reached these kids."

"God, I fucking hope so," I said, my mind going back to when I'd first met them. I'd worked hard to gain their trust. "This youth center is open to everyone but these kids are all LGBTQ, for the most part minorities and growing up poor. I want them to know they can have more than what is promised on the streets and that it gets better. Whatever shit is weighing them down now is just temporary."

"You grew up here?" he asked.

"Yeah, with my mom. I never knew my dad. He was dead before I was old enough to know that I didn't have one." I met his gaze, glad to see only interest and not pity. "I knew I was gay when I was fourteen and I buried it down deep because it would have gotten me killed on these streets. I was lucky enough to have this center, luckier to find hockey and it became my focus. I knew it was my only ticket out. I wasn't a great student and I didn't have any money."

"So, you want to come back here and help these kids?"

"I do. If I get the offer from the team here, I'll be able to do even more than send checks and fly in when I can."

He kept his eyes on me and I didn't want to break the connection. This was me, the complete unvarnished truth. I wanted him to see it and I wanted to see what he thought of me. If I was honest, it was why I'd invited him here. As dangerous as that could be for my sanity.

Etienne observed me closely and I wondered if he'd clue me into what he was thinking. He didn't disappoint.

"You're a good man, Jamie Washington and while I don't want the Rage to lose you, I hope you get an offer from the enemy." He dipped his chin and looked up at me through his dark lashes. It was a seductive gaze, whether he intended it to be or not. "You're not the guy I thought you were when you first joined the Rage."

"It took me long enough to get here," I answered, thinking of all the time I'd wasted hiding who I really was from everyone. How many times had I missed out because I was afraid? I didn't want these kids to do have to live that way.

"But you got here." He placed his hand on my shoulder, and gave it a squeeze. His fingers brushed against the bare skin just above the collar of my shirt and we both jumped, our eyes locking at the jolt of sensation. I took a deep breath, wondering if he could feel my pulse jumping just a fraction above where he rested his hand.

The doors burst open on the other end of the room and Dr. Carla Androghetti entered, her arms full of pizza boxes.

She was followed closely by two other volunteers with more pizzas and sodas.

"Cho! Co" Etienne said, his accent strong as he took in the sight. "That's enough food to feed an army."

"Or a bunch of teenagers," I said, glad to have his attention off me while I got my shit under control.

The kids swiveled on their heels, drawn by the smell of grease, cheese, and every kind of topping. A cheer went up from the crowd and they swarmed the food like they'd never eaten before. Or in the last hour. It was almost the same at their age.

Carla emerged from the crowd, laughing and holding a lone slice of something with lots of cheese on it. She took a bite, exaggerating her love for the slice as she teased the kids with it. Tyrique pretended to be hurt by her action but she gave him a light shove when he reached for the slice and then skipped away from the crowd and towards me.

I scooped her up into a hug when she got to me, dodging the slice of grease still clutched in her hand.

"That cup is huge," she said, looking towards Etienne for confirmation. "Am I right? Why does it have to be so big? I think it's because hockey players have small dicks. I'm a doctor, I know this kind of stuff." She nudged me with her elbow, not taking her gaze off the hot man standing next to me. "You going to introduce me?"

I ignored her jab at my manhood and rolled my eyes, making the back-and-forth motion between the two of them. "Dr. Carla Androghetti meet Dr. Etienne Beaufort."

"Psychiatry," she said, shaking his hand.

"Physical therapy," Etienne replied and then paused, his face scrunched up. "Wait. Are you Ryker's boss?"

Her smile remained on her face but she squinted at him for a few seconds and then understanding replaced the confusion. "Are you his best friend from New Orleans? The real-time, sexy

Cajun guy?" He nodded and she dropped the formality and hugged him, already deciding that this connection made them people who hugged. "It's a small world and Ryker was so right about you being hot."

I wracked my brain, trying to figure where I'd heard that name before and then it all made sense. Or I thought it did. The guy mentioned on the plane.

"*The* Ryker?" I asked.

"The one and only," Carla answered, drawing close to me for another one-armed hug. She was a toucher, the only way to stop her was to put a physical barrier in between the two of you. Like a wall. Or a continent. "He's my office manager. I know I've told you about him."

"The guy who pulled all the real estate listings for me?" And the ex-con who'd served a few years for killing a man. I'd checked into him as best I could when she'd hired him and while his past was rocky, he hadn't lied about it. I thought that counted for something and so far he'd been a stand-up guy to Carla.

"Yep." She tapped me on the chest before she backed away. "Don't forget, you owe him VIP tickets to a game." She nodded at Etienne. "It was nice meeting you. I've got to run back to the office."

"She's the best friend?" Etienne asked as we watched her leave the room, the kids grabbing last minute hugs along the way. They loved her.

"Yeah. I met her here at the center when we both started volunteering. She works with the kids, runs a boating program on the river for them and offers free counseling services."

"Ryker loves her."

"Well, so do I."

The kids didn't let the pizza slow them down. Hands full and fingers covered in cheese and sauce, they jockeyed to get their picture taken with the cup, their roughhousing and dirty fingers making Edwin twitch from his protective perch just to the right of the big hunk of metal. Etienne slid up next to me, handing over a paper plate with a slice of pizza on it. I took it and ate half of it in one bite. It wasn't half-bad for delivery pizza. I'd had better in Chicago but that was a whole other thing entirely. Nothing touched the level of a Chicago deep dish.

Etienne was beside me, laughing as J.J. shoved Tyrique out of the way in his effort to photobomb the picture. Rachel sat to the side, eyes wide as she watched her friends acting like bunch of idiots. She laughed at them, offering up a quiet comment into their round of jokes. Tyrique clutched his chest and fell to the ground, acting like she'd thrown a fatal blow. I snorted with a laugh and caught Etienne's attention.

"Who's that?" he asked.

I let out a sigh, sifting through what I felt comfortable sharing. Her full story wasn't mine to tell. "That's Rachel. A year ago she wouldn't have even been in this room much less joking with them. She's made a lot of progress, living her life fully as a transgender girl. She had a rough time there for a while."

I felt his hand on my arm and I turned to look at him. Etienne was staring at me, an expression of respect and affection on his face. I found myself smiling down at him, my heart rate kicking up at his attention. Every part of me liked that he was looking at me that way. Fuck, but he did it for me.

"What?" I asked, tossing my empty paper plate into the nearby trash can.

"They're the reason." He motioned towards the rowdy bunch making teenage asses of themselves in front of us. "The reason why you came out."

I nodded, letting my glance skip quickly over to the kids and then back to him. It was true. "I couldn't very well tell them to be proud of who they are if I was still hiding in the closet. They've had enough mixed signals and bad examples of being an adult from so many others. I wasn't going to be one of them."

I never saw it coming. But I didn't miss it when he moved closer to me, our arms and chests touching. There was barely any daylight between us and I ached to close even that distance. Etienne was right there, moving in to brush a light kiss over my lips before pulling back with a self-conscious look towards the kids and then back at me. It had happened so quickly they hadn't noticed. But I had. My whole body was on high alert. The adrenaline rush was higher than the moments before a game, those moments before I let my blade hit the ice and I flew.

This was a different kind of flying.

"You just keep getting better and better Jamie Washington," Etienne murmured, his tone low and sultry.

He studied me, his own expression neutral in spite of the pride and lust I saw in the depths of his brown eyes. I couldn't maintain the eye contact. It was making me self-conscious and horny. When he looked at me that way, I wanted him. But having a boner in front of the kids was a non-starter. Jesus, they'd never let me live it down.

Etienne didn't help me out when he brushed his warm hand over mine and gave my fingers a lingering squeeze. Nothing obvious and nothing over-the-top but enough to make me wish for more and a room not full of teenage kids. But, I did the grown-up thing and didn't touch him back and didn't drag him into another kiss. I deserved a fucking medal.

Or maybe just more time with this man.

"I have dinner with my agent and Carla later tonight but I was wondering . . ." I hesitated, digging deep to find my nerve. I faced down hundreds of pounds of fighting men every night on the ice. I could ask this guy out on a date. I smiled and went for it. "What are you doing tomorrow?"

DC

"You're never allowed to try to fix me up again."

Carla took the drink the waiter brought to the table and took a huge gulp as she eased back in her chair. I'd invited her to dinner with my agent Bryan, for moral support for me and to introduce her to a guy she might be interested in. The support part had worked out fine. The potential love connection? Not so much. I was going to pay for it. No good deeds and all that.

"I had no idea he'd been married four times," I said in my defense. "Why would I know that?"

"Jesus. How could you *not* know that?" She asked, her brown eyes huge with disbelief.

"He's my agent and we both have penises." I raised my hand to her, counting off on my fingers to make my point. "We talk about hockey and money. That's it."

"Look, everybody can make a mistake or four but that is not the guy who's going to be able to handle me. I need a guy with more fight in him. Four divorces to me screams that he gives up too easily. Don't give him my number if he asks for it."

Carla's current sex life consisted of serving as a third to

couples who wanted an extra participant in the bedroom. It wasn't that she didn't date one-on-one, she just wasn't willing to give up her extracurricular activities right now. Most of her solo partners had a problem with that and they didn't stick around very long. So, she wasn't wrong when she said he couldn't handle her.

"I'm not sure who *can* handle you but I look forward to meeting him," I thought about the complex woman sitting across from me and saluted her with my beer. "Or her."

Carla clinked her whisky glass against mine and took another drink, looking me over with the eye of someone who'd known me long and well.

"Etienne . . ." She let drawled his name out and I braced for impact. "So, you asked that sexy man out on a date? Good for you. It's about time you enjoyed your life out of the closet."

"I came out just before the season began and then I had no time to actually date," I defended my lack of love life for the past year.

"I'm not criticizing, I get it. You haven't had a ton of time for walks in the moonlight." Carla's lips twisted up in an evil grin. "Although, I hope you've had time for fucks in the moonlight."

I felt the heat hit my cheeks and I knew she could see it. Her level of sex positivity was at least six floors above mine. I wasn't a prude but when you spent most of your life making sure nobody knew who was getting you off, you weren't talking it about it so openly either. I had a lot of catching up to do. Or not.

"I got laid plenty but this is different." I sounded cliché but it was true.

"You like him."

"I might sound like a middle school girl but yeah, I like him." I took another drink and shook my head at my own stupidity. "Shitty timing to do something about it."

"The long-distance thing." What I liked most about Carla is that she got me and that meant I didn't have to do a lot of explaining. "If you get the offer, you'll be in two different cities."

"Yep. Long distance never works."

She screwed up her ace in disagreement. "Not true but let's say you're right. So, why ask him out now?"

I smiled to myself. That was an easy answer. "I'm looking for more and he makes me feel that . . . more."

She laughed and jumped up, coming around the table to plant a big, messy kiss on my face. I hoped her red lipstick wasn't the kind that stayed on during a nuclear holocaust. I wiped off my cheek and lightly shoved her away.

"What the fuck was that for?"

"Long distance is hard . . . not impossible." She leaned over to where phone sat on the table and tapped on it. "I'm going to the ladies and you're going to text 'Etienne-sexy-pants' and set up your date for tomorrow. Have fun. Flirt. Get laid. Worry about tomorrow when it gets here."

She walked away and I stared at the phone for a few seconds before I picked it up. This was dumb. I knew that there was no point. I was going to hang out with Etienne and unless he told me that he liked to kick puppies, I was just going to like him more. According to Bryan I was going to get a competitive offer from the DC team and that meant I would be moving to this city, one thousand miles from New Orleans and Etienne within the next month. This was terrible timing.

I picked up my phone anyway. I might be stupid but I wasn't crazy. I'd had a thing for Etienne since I'd first laid eyes on him. Carpe Diem and all that shit.

Me: Hey. You still want to play tourist tomorrow?
Etienne: I was wondering if you'd blow me off.
Me: No way. I'd like to play tourist with you.
Etienne: Can you handle ogling Daniel Craig's ass?

Me: Sure? Is he coming with us?

Etienne: Madame Tussaud's Wax Museum. Tackiest place on earth. You ever been?

Me: Nope.

Etienne: You'll love it. Meet at 10?

Me: I'm at the DuPont. Meet you there?

Etienne: Yeah. I'll be the one wearing the "I heart DC" t-shirt.

Me: I hope you're joking.

Etienne

"I know that smile isn't for me."

Ryker sat at the end of his couch, surrounded by the metric fuck ton of carbs we'd just consumed. He had a half marathon tomorrow so he needed the fuel. I had no excuse. I just ate all the things without stopping. I'd worry about a big gut when I got back to New Orleans.

I'd ignored his comment so he threw his napkin at me from where he sat and then lunged at me, grabbing for my phone. My arms were longer but he was bulkier and heavier with his boxer's body so while the struggle was real, it wasn't for long. I gave up, letting him have the phone. He launched himself back to his end of the sofa and thumbed across the screen and read my private messages. Ryker glanced up at me, the grin on his face wicked.

"*Embrasse moi tchew*," I grumbled, reaching for my beer and taking a long drink while I waited for him to give me shit about this.

"I have *no idea* what you just said."

"I told you to kiss my ass," I said. "You're a dick."

"I'll be the only one kissing it if you really wear that shitty t-shirt tomorrow. Nobody buys those things except tourists from the square states in the middle of nowhere," he said, tossing my phone back at me.

"*I'm* a tourist."

"With your very own, sexy tour guide," he said. "Carla says he's a great guy."

"He is." I settled back on the cushions, pressing my hand down on my overfull stomach. I shouldn't have had that second bowl of pasta. "I've known him since he started playing for the Rage but he was way in the closet and we didn't talk about it."

"You knew?"

"My gaydar is always right. You know this."

"Fuck off. You weren't right about that guy in Cancun." Ryker pointed at me, his frown fierce as he brought up old shit. "He was a great fuck but I'm not interested in popping the bi-curious cherry for a guy on weekend away from the wife and kids."

"That was years ago. Why do you keep bringing it up?"

"Because I don't want to talk about Oprah-shit like what you're doing with Jamie but I feel like I should." He rubbed his hand over his shaved scalp, the tattoo sleeve on his arm flexing as he moved. "I'm not going to go all emo or anything but I get the vibe that you like this guy and I'm just wondering what the fuck is going on."

Everything about him screamed that he would have been more comfortable having a lube-free cavity search at the local police department . . . and he would know. Ryker was a good friend but I wouldn't say that he was unequivocally a good man. He lived by his own code of right and wrong and that didn't always align with the world or, more specifically, the penal code. But he was my friend.

"I don't know what the fuck is going on," I said, getting up to grab another beer from the fridge. "I like him. He's beyond hot and he's interested." I thought back to our time on the plane and at the youth center. "He's great. It's fun. He's probably moving here within the next few weeks so it is what it is. It doesn't have to be anything."

"I know it doesn't have to be anything. I'm the crown prince of nothing but you're not." He motioned towards me from across the room as I emerged with the liquid courage necessary for where this conversation was going. "You're the king of joint mortgages, commitment, and Sunday dinner with your *Mamere.*"

I winced at him butchering my second-native tongue. It didn't change that fact that he was right. If I had a choice, I preferred to be with someone, to build a life with someone. I'd thought I had that with my last boyfriend but that had died a year ago. His choice. Not mine. And since then I'd avoided all that crap.

"Your cajun french is shitty. Just stop ruining it."

"Yeah well, my English is perfect so hear me now: stop dicking around and tell me that you know what you're doing. It's been a year since David moved out and I'm all over you getting your cock sucked as long as you know where your head is at."

"The big one or the little one?" I couldn't help but tease him. It was easier than having this conversation.

"Newsflash: the big one is currently up your ass. Mystery solved."

I flipped him the bird and leaned on the countertop. I was a little too buzzed to want to think about this so hard but the date was tomorrow. The date that would probably end up with Jamie and I naked and covered in sweat if I was reading it right. He'd get picked up here in DC and I'd head back to NOLA and carry around regret for a few months that this great guy couldn't be mine. What else could it be?

"It's a weekend thing. I'm not dumb enough to think this is going anywhere but I'll enjoy the ride."

DC

Daniel Craig's ass was drool-worthy even in wax.

Etienne and I stood side-by-side, checking out "007" from every angle. If the figures were as lifelike as they claimed, Mr. Bond would be a nice armful in bed. Tall enough, lean and covered in muscle. A man you could sink your teeth into.

Just like the man standing next to me wearing the ugliest fucking shirt I'd ever seen.

The shirt was black, a perfect choice to highlight the gold glitter "I 'heart" DC" logo scrawled across the front. It was tacky and cheap and Etienne wore it like a boss.

It only made me want him more. But it didn't stop me from busting his chops.

"That is an ugly fucking shirt," I said, reaching out to lift the back of the tuxedo jacket covering the statue to get a better look at the perfect curve of his ass. "And they should have put him in that bathing suit from 'Die Another Day'."

"Fuck off my shirt is amazing."

"Fine. But I'm right about the speedo."

"You're an idiot." Etienne said as he moved further along in the museum. Every celebrity you could think of was in this place and the waxwork was unbelievably lifelike. He stopped in front of Chris Hemsworth and looked at me, sizing us up. He pulled me into a position right next to the statue and then stepped back, making me squirm under his examination.

"You two are about the same size but I was never much into blondes. Grab his hammer."

"Okay, I know we're allowed to touch the statues but I'm pretty sure *that* will get us kicked us out of here," I joked, laughing harder when he scowled and flipped me the bird. I did as he said, pretending to try and lift Thor's weapon as he snapped a pic. I stepped forward to see what it looked like on the screen of his phone. His warmth drew me closer as I peeked over his shoulder, resting my chin against it. "So, you're not into blondes?"

Etienne shivered a little when my breath danced along the exposed skin of his neck and I grinned to myself, loving the reaction. We'd eased into a comfortable place, sharing physical space, mutually understanding that we enjoyed touching each other. The tease was enjoyable, almost innocent in spite of the spark of attraction that arced between the two of us.

It was as if we'd silently agreed to enjoy this day. Like we were in a bubble of only the "here and now". No offer pending from DC. No job back in New Orleans. Just us. I was willing to go with it.

"No." He shook his head, thumbing through the pics on his phone as we both pretended to actually look at them. All I could see was him. Even with James Bond only a few feet away. "I'm into brunettes. Dark hair. Olive skin."

So . . . guys who look like me. Good to know.

A family tromped into the room with us, the kids squealing at the sight of Captain America standing in the corner next to Thor and several other superheroes. We moved apart but our hands brushed in the process and I reached out on impulse, tangling our fingers for the briefest moment before letting him go. He flashed a smile at me and reached out, hooking a finger through as belt loop on my short and dragged me with him.

"What kind of guy are you into?" He asked as we walked down a hallway of sports figures. Babe Ruth. John McEnroe. Michael Phelps wearing a swimsuit. Bonus. He paused and flicked a questioning gaze at me. "You've had boyfriends before? I'm not sure how closeted you were." And then he dropped his hand from my waist and waved me off. "That was so fucking personal. You don't have to tell me."

I caught up with him, mimicking him by snagging his waistband to stop his retreat. When he turned to face me, I slid my hand down his forearm interlocking our fingers.

"I've never held hands with a guy in public. Never kissed a man out in the open. Dating? I'm a virgin. Behind doors and in the dark, I've done it all." I glanced over when the family form earlier joined us but I didn't let go of his hand. I'd risked everything to have a moment like this and I was going to take it. "You asked me why I came out and the biggest reason was the kids but it was also this. I was tired of hiding who I cared about and ashamed that I ever asked them to do it."

"I just can't imagine living like that," he said, shaking his head in emphasis to his disbelief. "I came out when I was in high school. I never had to hide who I was or who I loved."

"You're very lucky, then. I'm jealous." And suddenly all this heavy conversation was too much. I tugged him along to a room full of musicians and pop stars. At the entrance was Kylie Minogue, wearing very little. Her microphone was actually bigger than parts of her costume and I wondered how she had a clothing mishap when she danced around on stage. "Do I lose my gay membership card if I confess that I really don't like Kylie very much?"

Etienne laughed, dropping my hand to snap a photo. "David would have sold a kidney to go see her live."

I didn't need for him to explain who David was. I heard the

bare bones through the Rage rumor mill: they'd been together for two years and his lover had moved out for another man. Etienne had been subdued, a washed-out version of himself, during that time and I'd had no clue how to help him out. What advice could I give when I'd never been through it?

"Have you . . ." I stopped, unsure about what I wanted to ask.

"Been with someone since he left?" He nodded. "I've hooked up. I wasn't ready for anything else for a long time. He wrecked me and I'm man enough to admit it. I had a good time but as Ryker informed me, I'm a 'joint mortgage and Sunday dinner" kind of guy. I think I'm ready to maybe look for that again. To give it a shot." Etienne shrugged. "I never doubted that I wanted that someday. My *Mamere* says that love is the point of everything and I think I agree with her. At least it's been my dream for as long as I can remember."

I felt the pull of his words in my chest, somewhere that could only be my heart. What a weird fucking sensation. Weird but good. Suddenly all I wanted was to show him the only place I'd dared to dream.

"If you're a dreamer, then I've got the perfect place for you."

Etienne

The Planetarium at the Air and Space Museum was almost deserted.

Huddled down in the muddy darkness with Jamie, we watched the "sky" swirl over our heads. The universe, the galaxy and then the Washington, DC skyline unfolded over us with stars glowing like they were trying to show off. An elderly couple pointed to the ceiling as the recorded tone of a voice-over actor related to us all the constellations as they glowed especially bright in their turn.

Jamie sat beside me, his large body taking up more space than the small seat allotted to him. He spilled over the edges, broad shoulders, muscled arms and thighs rubbing up against my own with a delicious friction. I leaned into him, enjoying the contact for what it was: pure pleasure for the sake of pleasure.

"This is not where I expected you to bring me," I said, watching the couple in front of us. Maybe in their eighties, they were wearing matching t-shirts similar to mine and we'd given each other the wave of solidarity when we'd filed into the room together. "But this is cool. I've never been here before."

He leaned back, resting his head on the back of the seat while he pointed to a spot just over our heads. Jamie whispered when he spoke, close to my ear with his warm breath tickling the skin on my cheek.

"In Southeast DC where I grew up, there were too many lights to really see the stars in the sky. I didn't even realize how fucking bright and beautiful it all was until we came here for a school trip. The planetarium blew my mind. No joke."

His smile was bright white against the dark of his beard and the lighter dusk of his skin. Eyes the color of smoke glowed with his simple delight in being here. His joy made my breath catch. He was . . . stunning.

"I would come here when I couldn't figure shit out," he returned his gaze to the ceiling but I could still see the grimace that twisted his sexy lips. "I came here a lot when I figured out that I was gay because that shit rocked my world. It was hard enough being the only half-white kid in my neighborhood but adding queer into the mix was a quick way to get myself hurt. Or killed."

"So, you came here and dreamed? About . . .?"

His expression morphed back into a smile, softer than his usual bright grin but still gorgeous. "Escaping. Getting out of here and to a place where I could be who I was and not give a fuck about what other people thought about me. This was my dreaming place."

He reached out and took my hand and my heart stuttered at this man's simple seduction. Jamie wasn't the typical professional hockey player. He was quiet, spent a lot of his down time at the rink reading, didn't hit the party scene looking for puck bunnies.

I watched him now, not the stars unfolding overhead of us. Figuring out this man was far more interesting, a puzzle that kept adding layers as I placed pieces that I thought I knew.

Forget the galaxy. . .the final frontier was this man's heart for whoever was lucky enough to get him.

I moved in closer and Jamie turned his head to look back at me. Physically, we'd been closer but right now it felt like our souls were aligning somehow. My *Mamere* would say that it was chemistry, the pull of our souls together and for once I wouldn't argue. That's exactly what it felt like.

And then all that was swirling between us took off like a rocket seeking the distant stars when he closed the distance and kissed me. His mouth was warm, tongue wet and the heavy weight of his palm wrapped around the back of my neck was sizzling. I opened up to him immediately, starving for every taste, every lick, every graze of sharp teeth on my tender skin.

I reached up and wove my fingers with his own, holding him in place as the kiss went on and on. The lights came up gradually and I realized that the soothing voice piped in through the speakers had stopped and now the drone of the museum docent instructed us to leave through the door on the other side of the room.

Jamie released my mouth, his own lips wet from our kiss but he kept his hand in place, refusing to relinquish the connection. I found myself smiling at him and I know I had to look like an idiot but this guy made me happy. He made me laugh and he was honest and kind and seemed incapable of playing games. After a year of only knowing guys long enough to drop trou and slap on a condom, I really didn't want this to end when we left this room.

"Look, I know that this has a shelf-life. I'm going back to New Orleans and you're going to stay here and starting anything right now is such a bad fucking idea," I said.

"But . . .?"

"But I don't want to end this right now. I'm here for the weekend. You're here for the weekend . . ." I trailed off, asking him with my silence to meet me halfway. I didn't think I'd read him the wrong way.

"We can just have this weekend? Be grown-ups at the end and walk away?" Jamie asked.

"I can if you can," I said and then realized that it sounded like I could take it or leave it. That was not the case at all. "I want to and I hope you do too."

He let go of my neck, the warm slide of his palm across my skin leaving goosebumps in its wake. I shivered a little, enjoying the sensation of arousal and need. I felt alive.

"I want that too," he answered, his smile back in full force and prompting one of my own. "So, what are we going to do for the rest of our weekend?"

I wasn't sure how well my suggestion would go over. It had been a place where David and I had not met with a mutual enjoyment and it had been a rough spot on our relatively smooth relationship. In the end, there had really been no drama when we'd imploded. There'd never been enough fireworks to cause that kind of explosion on impact.

Me and Jamie? We had a mini-earthquake every time we touched.

"How do you feel about dancing?"

DC

_____

"The Club" was the name of the place where we met Etienne's friends.

A two-story venue, the bar was on the first floor and wide steps led to the second level dance floor. Techno pop blared from the speakers as a sea of hot guys of every make, model and size gyrated under the strobe lights. Almost all of them were shirtless and the sight of all that naked, hard sweaty flesh got my blood pumping in my veins in a straight line to my cock.

Ryker popped up into my line of sight. I wouldn't say that he grinned. It was much too feral for that but I think the flash of his teeth meant that he was happy about being here. It was hard to tell with the mask of nothing that usually covered his face.

"Is this the first time you've been to a gay club?" He asked.

"Since I've been out? Yeah." My only forays into gay clubs had been under the shadow of being found out and had shoved me into a back room with a nameless guy's mouth wrapped around my dick. To walk in the front door and sign autographs for fans? This was a first.

"Well fuck, man." Ryker threw an arm around my shoulder and gestured to the mob in front of us. "This is an all-you-can-eat buffet. I hope you're hungry."

He let go of me and started walking backward into the crowd. The last I saw of him was a glimpse of his six-pack and tons of tattoos as he took off his shirt.

Etienne appeared to my right, his afro was free tonight and I was itching to get my hands on it. At least I was until he grabbed the hem of his shirt and lifted it over his head, exposing the long expanse of his torso. Smooth brown skin, hair dusting over his pecs and down his treasure trail, a six-pack he worked hard to maintain.

I clenched my hands at my sides, an automatic gesture created by years of hiding my true desires but Etienne was having none of it. He reached over and grabbed my own shirt, forcing my arms up with his movement to remove the garment until my chest was bare to the heat of the room.

He ran his fingers over my body, lingering for a tantalizing moment on my right nipple before going lower. I sucked in my breath as his arm slipped around my waist and he pulled me tight against him. I wasn't the only one who was hard.

His breath was hot against my neck as he said in my ear. "Tonight you can touch as much as you want. Don't worry about anything. Just go with what you feel."

I let him lead me into the crowd and for the next couple of hours, I did exactly what he said. I felt. Everything. I felt like me. The real me.

The crowd moved together as one, bodies gyrating as song after song spun out through the invisible speakers. Men moved in and out of our circle. Some grabbed my interest: athletic men with hair on their chests, tattoos and a promising bulge. Other men, attractive younger guys with hairless bodies and guyliner, pressed against me in harmless flirtation. They were pretty but too fragile to get my blood going but they were fun.

But always within arm's length or in my line of sight was Etienne. He had a dancer's body and moved like pure sex, his movements like sultry strokes to my cock. I was more like that guy in "Footloose" – not Kevin Bacon, the other guy – I gave it my best but it was more like Frankenstein's monster than Solid Gold Dancer.

Etienne slid up to me, our sweat-slick chests sliding against each other as he wrapped an arm around my waist. He ground his groin against mine and I groaned, dropping my forehead to rest on the sweet spot where his shoulder met his neck. He smelled of clean, male sweat and his favorite aftershave. I bit down lightly, smiling when his body jumped, grinding even closer against me.

I watched Ryker dance with a slender blonde a few feet away. The man was beautiful, tall but slim, platinum hair messed like he'd just rolled out of bed, his makeup perfectly applied. They stared at each other, bodies moving together but their expressions didn't match the exuberance of the crowd around them. They looked. . . complicated.

Etienne caught the direction of my gaze and shook his head. He leaned back in so that he could speak directly in my ear. "That's a fucked up thing right there. Ryker and his rent boy. Not gonna end well."

"That kid?" I took another look at him. He couldn't be a day over twenty-years-old.

"That kid pulls in more in a night than I get paid in a week." Etienne looked back at me, his grin wicked as his hand drifted down to stroke my cock through my jeans. "You can have me for free."

I half-laughed, half-groaned as his hand cupped my dick. I fucked into his grip wanting. . .more. He gave it to me.

His mouth was hot, his tongue wet as it slid against my own in a struggle for dominance. The kiss at the center had been barely a butterfly breath. The one at the planetarium sexy but sweet. This was feral, needy. This kiss promised that I'd end up with my come down his throat or spilling across his chest at some point tonight.

We kept moving together, our mouths tasting everywhere we could reach. Stubbled jaws, sensitive pulse points on our necks, salty skin on our shoulders. I moved to the beat of the music and the throb in my cock, enjoying the freedom of doing what I wanted with no worry.

And then other hands and mouths joined our own. The crowd swirled around us and men moved in and out of our orbit, their hands coasting over my skin, squeezing my ass and briefly joining Etienne's where he claimed my dick. Lips brushed kisses over the back of my neck as I explored Etienne's mouth with my tongue, a finger teased my nipple before it disappeared and left me aching with desire.

Etienne broke off the kiss and I opened my eyes, dazed and foggy from the lust burning through my system. This was hot but there was only one man I wanted so I followed him when he took my hand and led me through the crowd towards the back of the club.

I'd expected him to lead me into the restroom where we could find a stall and maybe jerk each other off before returning to the dance floor but he passed it by. Instead he walked down a dimly lit hallway just beyond. We turned a corner and entered a space full of men. Kissing, touching, on their knees, fucking. It was hard to take it all in but I tried.

Etienne pulled me into an alcove, not private but off the main walkway and backed me up against the wall. His gaze was hot, his hands roving over my skin as he watched my expression. No doubt gauging my comfort level.

"This okay?" he asked, nipping at my bottom lip and then my jaw before catching my gaze again. "Anything you want. We can go or we can stay."

There was no fucking way we were leaving. I looked

around the space, watching the men as they moved against each other in pairs and threesomes and I inhaled the scent of arousal in the air. This wasn't my first back-room rodeo but it was the first time I knew the guy's name and I wasn't ashamed to be here. I wasn't fucking going anywhere.

"I want you to suck me off," I said, but my tone made it more of a demand. He smiled and leaned in closer.

Etienne's tongue was hot against my neck, and his hands were busy at the fly of my jeans. I leaned against the wall while he sank down to his knees—and damn, looked up at me through his thick fringe of dark eyelashes. It was hot, his opening my pants to get at my cock while I watched him watching me. He was going too slow.

"C'mon. You got me hard and now you're dicking around," I said. "I know you want it. I can see it on your face so stop dawdling and put your mouth on me."

Etienne pinched my nipple and arousal zinged down my spine to my groin.

"I'm going to take my time and you're gonna deal with it," he said, his voice dark and firm. "Just sit back and watch while I get you off."

I liked that he pushed back, it made my dick even harder and my need went feral. I grabbed his hair, jerking his head back to make him maintain contact while he exposed my cock. He pulled down my jeans, over my hips and I bucked them in invitation. He grinned up at me, his mouth hovering so close to where I needed it that I felt the warm rush of air against my balls. I groaned, my eyes sliding shut until I felt his fingers pinch my nipple again. The pain was sweet and my cock got harder, swelling where it pressed against my stomach, begging for attention.

He settled back on his heels and it didn't look like he was going to follow my order anytime soon so I let go of his hair and took my cock in hand, rubbing it against his cheekbone.

He moaned, no words just a rough sound as he arched into the caress. His hands ran up the outside of my thighs, crossing over to tease the inside of my thighs and my balls. I shifted my stance, widening my legs as I pumped my cock slowly, jerking myself off against his face.

He slipped a finger behind my balls, teasing me and promising that I'd get the ass action I craved. I could switch it up in the bedroom but I loved bottoming. The fullness of cock inside me made me wild. There was never anything better. I gave my cock a few more pulls and then opened my legs as far as they would go, giving him all the access I could with my jeans pooled at my ankles.

I watched as he slid his fingers into his mouth, getting them good and wet before he slid them higher up my crack and then pressed one in, slowly but firmly. I sighed and angled my hips out giving him room to push another finger inside me, deeper this time as he searched for my sweet spot. He found it and my knees buckled, my hand faltering in the rhythmic pulls on my cock as I looked down at Etienne's face. He got off on this, his pupils were blown, cheeks ruddy and lips red from where he was biting them.

I wasn't going to last long at this rate.

"Suck it." I shoved my cock against his face and he opened wide, sliding his hot, wet mouth all the way down. I unclenched my free hand and slid it into hair with the other one and held him in place. I didn't fuck into his mouth but I wanted to. Instead, I let him suck me down into his throat, catching my breath when he did this fluttery thing that hit the underside of my cock head and made me see stars.

"I'm going to come," I warned him, giving him a chance to release me and let me finish on his face or on the floor. I didn't give a fuck where. But Etienne didn't back off. He sucked me harder and wrapped his free hand around my ass cheek and took his turn at holding me in place while sliding his finger in and out of my hole.

The next time he deep-throated me his knuckle pressed on my prostate and I could barely breathe. It felt so fucking good and I gave into it. My whole body arched against Etienne's face, his head in my hands, and every muscle clenched tight while I shot down his throat.

He kept me in his hot, wet heat, sucking me gently as I came down from my orgasm-high. I was getting too sensitive so I pushed him off and pulled him to his feet, capturing his mouth as I reached for the fly on his jeans. He took the kiss, tasting of my come and Etienne but he stopped me from taking his cock in my hand.

"You don't want me to get you off?" I asked, pulling back in confusion.

"Not here," he leaned in for another kiss. It was gentler but no less hot. "I want to fuck you"

I always liked a man who got to the point, especially when we were on the same page.

"Let's go."

Etienne

Jamie's suite was dark but I didn't care.

All I needed to know is where the bedroom was and if he had a condom and lube. I could totally handle it from there.

"I've got an *ahnvee* for you Jamie," I said, my voice thick with lust and my accent. "I want to eat you up. The taste at the club was not enough."

We were all kisses and touches and shaky fingers as we stumbled across the floor and into the bedroom. Jamie broke away from me for a second and flipped on the light, bathing the room in a warm glow. He turned to me dropping the last of his clothing to the floor and my progress stalled as I soaked him in. This wasn't the first time I'd seen him naked but the want on his face, the need making his muscles taut and his fat, blunt cock hard for me almost brought me to my knees again.

"Show me," he said, gesturing towards my jeans. "I'm dying to see you Etienne."

I shoved my jeans and briefs down and kicked them away, straightening so that he could get his fill. His eyes were so dark, pupils dilated with his arousal and they raked over me from head to toe and then back again. When he met my gaze, he smiled like a kid who'd found his favorite gift under the tree.

Two long strides brought him back to me and he wasted no time taking my mouth in a hard, urgent kiss. It was all tongue and teeth and groans as we pressed against each other, naked and sensitive. His hands roamed all over and I no sooner felt relief at him touching me in one place when another spot ached for his attention. I could not stay still, my body writhing against his. His large hand wrapped around my cock made me gasp.

"Fuck, Jamie." My head lolled back, exposing my neck to his trail of kisses and nibbles and licks. He rolled his palm over my leaking tip and then used my pre-come as lube, making his glide smooth from root to tip. My hips moved in his grip, seeking that friction that would get me off. But this isn't what I wanted.

I pushed him away, edging him back towards the bed. He watched me, eyes wide and feral as he waited to see what I would do.

"On the bed. Ass up. I want to see your hole."

He blinked. One long, slow sweep of lashes while I watched an aroused flush travel across his chest and cheeks. But he didn't hesitate, turning and climbing onto the bed, stopping only with his exposed ass in the air while his face rested on his folded arms. I groaned. This was going to be fun.

I moved behind him, letting my hands roam all over his back, his thighs, underneath to tweak his hard nipples and then I indulged in the hard, firm globes of his ass.

"You have such a beautiful body, Jamie. So beautiful, *cher*." It was the honed instrument of an athlete and I'd seen first-hand what he had trained it to do. Powerful, I was dying to have all of that strength quivering underneath me.

I squeezed his ass again, trailing my fingers over his hole, caressing the nerves bundled there. He groaned, long and deep into the covers, his fists balling the fabric as he pushed back into my touch. I lowered my head and took my first taste of him there, dark and male. The sensation went straight to my head, making a little dizzy with my own lust as I tongued-fucked him and he went wild underneath me.

He shoved back against my mouth, begging for more with his actions and I was happy to oblige him. I reached over to the bedside table and grabbed the lube he'd stashed there.

"So, you thought I was a sure thing?" I asked as I drizzled the glossy liquid over his crack and my fingers.

"Nope," he gasped as I inserted a finger, pressing inside his heat. "I knew I would be if I got you back here."

His answer deserved an award so I slid in another finger, gently loosening the muscles around the rim. Jamie groaned again, jolting when I brushed his prostate once . . .and then again when his reaction made my cock even harder. He lunged back towards me, taking my fingers even deeper and so I added a third, watching his back muscles ripple at the combination of burning pain and pleasure I knew he was experiencing. His entire body undulated under me as I leaned over him, fucking him slowly and driving him crazy.

"Etienne, come on fuck me. You own this ass, just take it," he growled as he lifted his head and twisted to the side, taking my mouth in a sloppy, wet kiss. It took a lot for me to pull away from him, all hot and sweaty and obedient under me but I wanted to be inside him. Not as if I'd die from the denial of if but that I'd never know what living was really like if didn't give into it.

I reached over and snagged a condom, quickly and efficiently rolling it on and lubing it up. Then I pulled in close behind him and with a kiss to his left shoulder blade, I pressed the tip of my cock to his hole. That first resistance was a sweet thing, sending shivers up my spine but the second push gave me that tight squeeze on the head that made my eyes cross.

One more retreat and another gentle push and I was inside him, throwing my head back in pleasure at the tight, hot clutch of him around me.

Jamie panted beneath me, his chest heaving and I gave him a moment to catch up, reaching around to stroke his cock as he adjusted to my invasion. He was hard, wet-tipped and hot to the touch and I remembered how perfectly he filled my mouth and throat. So fucking good.

"You good?" I whispered against his neck, pressing soft kisses there as his body relaxed underneath me. When he gave a nod and pressed back against me, I began to move.

Tight and hot. That's all I could think of as I pressed in and out of his ass. Each pass bringing me closer and closer to my own climax. I'd barely been able to resist coming in my jeans at the club but with him naked, open and surrendered to me like this, I knew I wouldn't last long.

I glanced up and caught our reflection in the mirror covering the closet doors.

"Look at us, *cher*."

I bit his shoulder to get his attention, slowing down my thrusts once his gaze met mine. His skin, although olive in tone was lighter than my own but they both glistened with sweat. My longer leaner body was able to stretch across his back, placing our faces close enough to kiss. I leaned down and pressed a soft kiss to his jaw, loving the way his eyes stayed locked with mine as I sped up my strokes.

I was getting close and I needed Jamie to be there with me.

"Jerk yourself off. I'm so fucking close and I want to be inside you when you come."

He obeyed my command, supporting himself on one hand as he reached underneath with the other. I had the best seat in the house when I lifted off him and began my hard thrusts from behind. I could see his face and the way his hand stroked his hard, thick cock and then I could feel him as he began to fuck himself on me, pressing back every time I lunged forward.

I reached forward and grasped his shoulders in my hands, the extra leverage allowing me to go deeper and to hit is sweet spot on each downward plunge.

"Oh my God, Etienne," Jamie cried, his body tensing underneath me the split second before white jets of come spilled out between his fingers and onto the coverlet. His body clutched me tight and I sucked in a huge gulp of air before my own release rolled through me like the fucking levees breaking in NOLA. Riptide. Undertow. Wave after wave.

"*Cher*," I groaned out, meaning every part of the endearment down to my soul in that moment.

My ears buzzed with the rush of blood in my system and I struggled to pull air into my lungs. Jamie collapsed, shifted forward to lie flat on the bed and I went with him, unwilling to give up our connection. He was warm underneath me, his muscles relaxed and pliant as I molded my body to his. I didn't want to move but my softening cock reminded me that I needed to take care of a few things.

I kissed his shoulder and eased myself out of his body, tying off the condom and tossing it in the bathroom trash. I wet a washcloth with warm water and walked back to the bed where my lover was sprawled just where I left him. The first touch of the cloth against his ass caused him to raise his head and look at me over his shoulder.

"You just relax, I'm gonna take care of you," I said, rolling him over to wipe the cooling evidence of his good time off his chest before tossing the cloth the floor. Then I settled myself over him, joining our mouths in a deep kiss.

"You can own my ass anytime you want," he sighed into the kiss, our light laughter breaking it off entirely. "Seriously, that was a great fuck."

"Good to know," I said, looking down at him. I should

probably roll over and let the guy get some sleep but I didn't want to stop touching him yet. "I had a great time this weekend, Jamie."

What I left unsaid was how fast it had flown by, how I wanted more of it, more of him. I couldn't believe just how badly our timing sucked.

"What is it you say? *Bad locque?*" He tried to put a Cajun spin on the whole thing but it sounded more like a guy with his mouth full and bad speech impediment. But I got what he was trying to say. It wasn't us and it wasn't that we didn't work. It just was what it was.

Bad locque.

DC

W aking up to my phone ringing was not ideal.

I was warm, draped over Etienne's strong, naked body coming to a sort of doze with a case of morning wood. I had ideas about what to do with it which involved Etienne's mouth. They *did not* involve my agent calling me this early in the morning on a Sunday.

"Whoever that is, they better be calling to give you a million dollars," Etienne grumbled and rolled over, burying his head under one of the four hundred pillows the hotel put on the bed. Half of them were tossed all over the room, deposited there during our two rounds of athletic sex.

"Hang on a minute, Bryan," I mumbled into the phone as I searched the floor for my jeans. I grabbed them, finding them lying in a pile next to Etienne's pair, and slid them on over my bare ass as I headed for the living room area of the suite. I glanced back over my shoulder, soaking in the sight of him sprawled across the mattress. His dark skin was in deep contrast with the white sheets, the lean muscles of his back, legs and ass on mouth-watering display. I was coming back to taste that all over again - as soon as I was done with this telephone call.

"Yeah, I'm here," I said as I pulled the door behind me. "What's up?"

"They gave you everything, DC. You got goddam everything you asked for." Bryan's voice had an edge of excited hysteria that I was sure would get him kicked out of the agent club. "Fuck, you could've asked to sleep in the Lincoln bedroom with four hookers and they'd given it to you."

"What?" I was fuzzy, not sure I heard what he said.

"Wake up man! I said they gave you fucking *everything*."

My legs went wobbly, as if I'd just been through a grueling practice session, and I sank down on the couch in shock. My ass hurt a little but not enough to make me regret last night. I leaned forward, rubbing my hand over my eyes as my head spun with the news and the residual effects of partying last night.

I heard movement in the other room, heard the shower turn on and knew Etienne was awake. The idea of him wet and naked in the shower was distracting and tempting but I needed to focus.

"I can't believe it. When are you going to tell the Rage?"

"I'll put the call in later today and we'll figure out a joint time to have a press conference. I know you want to do this right."

I thought over how much support I'd received from the Rage management, my teammates, my fans. It hadn't been easy but they'd stood by me when I'd needed it. I owed them the courtesy of making a smooth transition.

"Yeah, I do." I thought about all the plans I had for the kids at the Center, the programs I could get funded when I was here to fundraise for them full-time. And playing on the ice for my hometown . . . it was a dream come true. I bit back emotion, hot and raw where it burned in my throat. "Listen Bryan, thank you."

"It was my pleasure man. You're a dream client."

"You could have dropped me or worse when I insisted on coming out but you didn't. Thank you for that, man." I'd done something that could've dried up my income stream for good and his as well. He'd never even blinked. I was going slip him a bonus above and beyond his fifteen percent. With this deal, I could afford it.

"DC, enjoy this victory. You deserve it. I'll be in touch."

He hung up and I was left alone with my thoughts and adrenaline spiking through my veins. A year ago I wasn't sure if my career would be over. This was . . . insane. My eyes drifted to the door separating me from the one thing that dampened my excitement. My coming out had been because I wanted to live a full life. A complete life. A life with someone like Etienne.

So many guys were like the ones at the club last night. Looking for fun and hard dick and that was it. There was nothing wrong with that. I just wanted more and it was a son-of-a-bitch that the guy I'd like to try it with was going to be living one thousand miles away.

I leaned back on the couch and closed my eyes, running scenarios of how it could work and I always came back to the same conclusion that this was the wrong time, wrong place but the right guy. Not a formula for success.

The door opened and I watched as Etienne exited the bedroom and strolled into the living room of the suite. Mocha brown skin still damp from his shower, he was dressed in the clothes he wore to the club last night . . . except for the addition of my t-shirt instead of his own. He looked good in my clothes and I didn't bother to tamp down the surge of possession that choked me at the sight.

I wanted Etienne. I just couldn't have him. It wasn't anyone's fault. Our timing just didn't work. It was *bad loque* - just as Etienne said.

He lowered himself into the space beside me of the sofa and slid closer when I draped my arm around his shoulders. We shifted against each other, trying not to lose contact as we found the perfect fit of our bodies together. Hard muscle and long limbs tangled in an intimate puzzle until we settled and he turned his head, meeting my gaze with his own.

"You got the deal," he said, his voice low and washing over me with that sweet bayou burr. It wasn't a question, we'd both known how this was going to end. "I'm so happy for you, Jamie." He tilted his head and scoured my face as if he was searching for a vital clue. "Aren't you happy?"

I searched his eyes and face for any sign of disconnect between his words and the truth of feelings but I knew I wouldn't find any. Etienne *was* happy for me. He cared about me and it was just one more indicator that this man was special, this man was what I needed in my life. He was the guy I had in mind when I'd decided to finally step out of the closet and vowed to live a life that made me happy.

But even though I knew all that, felt it down in my marrow, I had to speak the truth.

"I'm happy. It's exactly what I wanted," I corrected myself. "It's more money than I ever thought they'd give me. They gave me almost all of my demands. My agent is stunned."

"I'm not," he leaned in to kiss me lightly, his sexy mouth spreading into a wide smile against my lips. "They'd be crazy not to keep you."

And just as fast as it had arrived, his grin faded and the knowledge of what we could not have brought down the mood in the room. And the unspoken question of why he wasn't going to keep me . . . and vice versa.

"I don't know how we would make it work," I said,

throwing a huge spotlight on the questions silently pinging back and forth between us. I didn't expect him to have a solution but a part of me hoped that he would, that he was just waiting for me start the conversation. I didn't even try to ease back on the frustration hardening the edges of every one of my words. "I've never even had a long-term relationship so I don't know how to do this in-or-out of the same zip code."

"You're going to have so much on your plate. A new town. The kids at the center, a new job . . ."

"I know it's not the right time. "

"I wish it was," he whispered. "But it isn't."

And there was really nothing else to say. We both knew that this was not the right time to start this. Long distance was a bitch and I had no idea what my new life was going to look like. No idea if it had room for Etienne.

"*Cher* . . ."

I used the word he'd spoken in the dark last night, against my skin, sighed into a kiss, shouted on the wave of his coming. I didn't say it with the same sexy, lilt of NOLA as Etienne but all I was feeling made up for it.

Leaning in I took his mouth, wasting no time to press my tongue inside and taste the now-familiar spice of Etienne. It wasn't the hungry kiss of last night but it was just as hot. Just slower and deeper as we lingered over saying goodbye.

He moaned and wrapped his hand around my neck, pulling me down and allowing not even a breath of distance between us. I surrendered to his demand because it mirrored my own want. I couldn't believe I was voluntarily walking away from this man. I was a total moron. It was the right thing to do but also epically stupid. The only thing that made it bearable was the knowledge that he was feeling the same thing.

We broke apart, panting breaths and swollen mouths and a metric fuck-ton of regret on our shoulders. When he rose from the couch and walked to the door to head down to catch a ride back to Ryker's place, I had to know.

"Hey, you regret any of this weekend?"

He smiled, the big one that I liked to think was just for me. "Not a minute of it."

And then he walked out and I let him go.

Etienne

"How was your Uber ride-of-shame?"

I stopped my supposedly stealthy progress through Ryker's apartment, swiveling my head to find him sitting at the bar in his kitchen, coffee cup in hand and a smirk on his face. He was in a pair of running shorts, chest bare, tattoos covering most of the skin and hiding the scars he rarely talked about. One night, with a full bottle of tequila shared between us, I'd heard his story and learned to hate a man I'd never met and to admire the son I was grateful to know.

"I'm guessing you had a good time because I would swear that you left wearing a different shirt." He squinted and craned his neck as if he needed to get a better look at me and what I was wearing. Dick. He saw me and my clothes just fine. "Wait? Wasn't DC wearing a shirt just like that last night? Were you so exhausted from fucking and sucking all night that you forgot what you wore?" He let out a fake laugh. "I want to get laid like *that*."

"Fuck off," I said. There was no heat behind my words and *that* got his attention. Ryker rose from his perch, poured a second mug and slid it across the bar to me.

"That's the best you've got?"

"Yeah. That's all I've got." I groaned out loud as I took my first sip of the brew. Black, strong and a little bitter, Ryker knew how I liked my coffee. I debated lying about the reason but that wasn't me. Not with my one of my oldest friends. "I left it all in Jamie's hotel room."

That got me a look and few long beats of silence while he considered my words. His expression morphed from confusion to understanding tinged with a little bit of pity. Normally that would piss me off but I'd take it from Ryker. He didn't feel sorry for me, he just knew that the situation sucked.

"So, he got the offer?"

"Yep."

"And you guys are . . . ?"

I chewed on that question for a minute, covering up my delay with another sip of coffee. Ryker waited, never a guy to fill a silence and let you off the hook.

"Friends."

"With benefits? Long distance booty call? Phone sex buddies?" He cocked his head and flashed a grin at me. "Clandestine meetings at an airport bathroom glory hole during hockey season?

"Where the fuck are you getting laid these days?"

"This is not about where *I* get my dick sucked," he waved me off and u-turned the conversation right back to me. "This is about you and a guy you couldn't keep your eyes off of last night. You two clicked. Everyone saw it. Am I wrong?"

"Long distance never works." I ignored his question because in the end it didn't matter how well Jamie and I fit together. Ryker wasn't letting it go.

"That's bullshit and you know it's bullshit because you're using it to avoid answering my question." He nailed me with a glare of frustration and repeated his question again. Nice and slow. "Am. I. Wrong?"

I slid off the stool and walked over to the large double doors leading out to his tiny balcony. Through the glass I could see people walking and enjoying the gorgeous summer day in Dupont Circle. Washington in the summer reminded me of New Orleans in some ways. Areas of it were always teeming with people, walking their dogs, eating at outdoor cafes, and enjoying the weather and the energy of the city. I remembered how awesome it had been to play tourist with Jamie yesterday, how well we'd "clicked". He was smart, kind, funny and crazy sexy. Everything I thought he'd be, turned out to be true. He was better actually.

"I think I could love Jamie," I said, putting the truth out there once and for all. Saying it didn't give it power or anything, it couldn't change a damn thing. Geography, jobs, obligations, distance. A four-letter word didn't change any of that.

"So what's the problem?" I could hear the ceramic thud of his coffee mug on the counter across the room and I knew he was gearing up to let me have it. "Etienne you aren't one of those guys who want an endless stream of tricks running in and out of your bed. Yeah, you like to have a good time in the back room of club as much at the next red-blooded gay man but in the end you prefer being with one guy, making something real."

"It's hard to make something real with over a thousand miles in between you."

"It's hard but not impossible."

I turned to face him, reiterating all the reasons why this was a non-starter. They were all true and they all made perfect sense. "He's going to be learning a new team in a new town. He's got the kids at the center and everything he wants to do there. He just came out . . ."

"And you don't want to stand between him and the smorgasbord of gay hockey fan ass he'll want to try out now that he's wearing a rainbow flag on his helmet?"

"Well . . . yeah." I said it but I didn't like it. I didn't really believe it though. Jamie didn't seem to be looking for that at all. He also wanted something real and that's why this sucked so fucking much.

"You're so full of shit," he growled and strode across the room to go at me nose-to-nose. There was tension in his posture and heat in his words but there was no fight in his eyes. He wasn't mad. He was . . . disappointed. "Don't be like me."

"What are you talking about?" Ryker was one of the best people I had in my life. I could always count on him to tell me the truth, whether I wanted to hear it or not. If I needed him, he was there. He'd had my back in fights and to be like him wouldn't be a bad thing.

"I fuck around all the time and I love it. The dirtier the better. I don't have stupid rules about not doing the same guy twice; if we're having a good time I keep them around until we're not. It's easy and fun but its not real." He paused, taking a deep breath before he plowed forward. "I don't even let myself take the chance. I just shut it down. I don't even try. To try would take too much work and bring up shit I don't want to deal with." I opened my mouth but he kept going, deliberately cutting off the denial I was going to voice. "You *try*. You put yourself out there and I think that is so fucking cool. You get knifed in the back and disappointed and hurt but you try anyway. You're a fucking badass. Don't be like me."

I didn't know what to say. I stared at him, one of my best and oldest friends and let his words sink in. I think it was the most words he'd ever spoken at one time that wasn't fueled by liquor and I had no idea what do with them. They'd landed a little too close to my truth. I needed time to process, time away from Jamie and the imprint of his touch on my body, the smell of him on my skin, to get my head straight. This weekend had been too much, too fast.

And Jamie had never asked. I was a guy who went for what he wanted but this time I held back. Jamie had a lot of shit to figure out in a new town, new team, new life. If he'd been staying in New Orleans this would have been completely different.

I glanced around the room, looking for an escape and found it in the clock on the entertainment center.

"I've got to get ready to go to the airport." I moved past him, walking towards the guest room. I had just enough time to pack my stuff and make my flight. Ryker moved back to the kitchen behind me and I paused before I headed down the hall, looking back over my shoulder. "Thanks for the advice. Working at Dr. Androghetti's office is rubbing off on you."

"I'll send you my bill." He saluted me with his coffee mug. "Now go pack your shit and I'll take you to the airport." He smirked. "Unless you want me to drive you back to DC's hotel."

I just turned and walked away because deep down that's what I really wanted to do.

DC

"The kids are still talking about you bringing by 'the cup'. That seriously made their year."

I turned towards the entrance to the boat house to find Carla silhouetted against the backdrop of the sun glittering on the water of the Anacostia River. She was gorgeous, her smile huge and her hair tumbling from a messy pile on top of her head. Wearing and old t-shirt and shorts, you'd never guess that she was the most sought after shrink in DC and held the secrets of our nation's rich and powerful.

I was getting ready to hand over some of mine.

"I wouldn't have missed it for the world," I answered, letting the memories of their excitement bring a smile back to my face. When my agent asked if I would have taken less money to move to Washington, I'd said yes with them in mind. "I love those kids."

"Don't let them know that," she joked as she walked into the boathouse and dumped a load of equipment on a nearby bench. "They'll use it to their advantage and you'll be screwed."

"It's too late."

"Well, then . . . it was nice knowing you, *suckah*," Carla teased, turning her back to me as she sorted her crap into several labeled bins attached to the wall.

I let her work in silence, taking the time to figure out my own shit a little bit better. When she was done, she grabbed two bottles of water from a nearby dorm-sized fridge and tossed one in my direction. I reached out to catch it but the condensation-slick plastic juggled between my palm and fingers and I let out a string of colorful curses before I finally captured it against my chest.

"It's a good thing you play hockey and not football butterfingers," she laughed, returning my middle-finger salute with the added bonus of a fish-lipped kiss blown in my direction.

"Go fuck yourself," I grumbled with force but no heat, opening the bottle and letting the cold liquid coat my dry throat. It was hot as fucking balls outside and inside the boat house wasn't much better.

"Did you kiss Etienne with that mouth?" she asked, lifting the bottle to her lips but letting her movement stall when I didn't answer. She leaned in close and shoved my arm. "You *did*! You lucky dog. I want to know *everywhere* you kissed him. Did he top? I bet he's great with his hands."

"You have zero filter." I wasn't embarrassed or surprised. Carla's sexual preferences were decidedly left of the mainstream and she was the poster girl for "sex positivity". I couldn't keep the "I was fucked so good" grin off my face. "Fuck yeah. He's good with his hands, his cock. He *did not* disappoint."

She grinned and leaned in close again. "When are you going to see him again?"

"I'm not." I thought about the trip I'd have to make back to NOLA to pack my shit and the inevitable night of drunken goodbyes I'd have with the guys on the team. I'd invite Etienne but I wasn't sure if he'd come. After our morning conversation that seemed like a recipe for unnecessary emo moments. "We both agreed that it's a one-and-done."

She scowled, not liking where this was going. Join the club. "Wait. That's nuts. I saw more than just chemistry between the two of you. You didn't click outside of the boning?"

"We were good. Everything was good." I paused to think it through, to get the explanation right. "I got the offer I wanted. I'm moving back here."

"Fuck, yes!" She jumped up, hugging me tight and spilling water from her opened bottle down my back. I laughed, enjoying my happiness over the deal fly free and unshadowed by my situation with Etienne. "You can stay with me until you find your own place. I cannot believe we are finally going to be living in the same town."

"I can't promise that I won't drink out of the orange juice carton."

She pulled back and waved her fist at me, looking way too cute to be scary. "I'll cut you."

I shoved her away and settled back on the bench, reluctant to get back to the real conversation. "So, long distance is hard."

"And long distance is hard," she said, nodding in under-standing. She took a drink and then flung the open bottle at me, wetting down my front so that it would match the back. I threw my hands up, giving her a "WTF" look as I grabbed the bottle from her. "It's hard you idiot. Not impossible."

She was smarter than me. I knew it. She knew it. But I attempted to argue anyway. "Why would I do that to myself? I like him. I could really like him. But I know that shit isn't going to work and it's all going to blow up in my face down the line. Why fucking bother?"

She stared me down for a few seconds, her eyes sending the

signal that she thought I was a dumbass. "I'm going to assume the you've taken so many hits to head on the ice that it's made you stupid." I opened my mouth to protest but she slapped her hand over it to keep me quiet. "I make a fuck ton of money off people who are looking ways to get over regret. Regret over things they didn't say or do, the job they didn't take, the people they didn't take a chance on loving. It fucking breaks my heart every time. Don't live your life like that. Just don't."

Her hand slid off my face and down to her lap with a thud. She tucked a curl back into her ponytail and squared her shoulders like she dared me to blow her off with some kind of dumb joke. She didn't need to worry. I didn't have any.

I wanted Etienne. This weekend had not been enough. I didn't know what would be enough. Two weekends. Ten. Twenty. A lifetime of weekends. Jesus. My stomach clenched at the thought that I was missing something. That I was on the verge of missing something.

"It could all go to shit," I said.

"Yep." She agreed, her smile just a little too smug. "Or not."

Or. Not.

———

OF COURSE, the airport was busy.

Sunday was a big travel day and I cursed the crowds as I tried to quickly maneuver my big body past luggage and kids and old people. On the ice I would've just plowed through them all, sending them spinning like tops out of my way. Here it would only get me a rectal cavity search from a TSA agent so I moved through the crowds as politely as I could.

There were two flights to NOLA leaving at the time of Etienne's flight. I couldn't get down to the gate without a ticket so I had to grab him before he got beyond the security check point. I scanned the crowd, straining to see his tall frame above all the other people. It should have been easy but all it was frustrating. Maybe I should fly down to New Orleans?

I hadn't thought this through. Inspired by Carla's speech and the bone deep fear that I might end up on her fucking couch one day with this regret.

I'd taken off from the boat house, driven by a need to talk to Etienne and see if he was willing to take a risk too. Hoping that I would catch him before it was too late. It looked like I was too late.

"You going back to New Orleans to pack up your stuff?"

I closed my eyes. His voice was sticky with the dark, deep secrets of the bayou. Sexy as hell with a hint of humor that made me smile as I turned to face him. His hair was loose today, the afro eye-catching and his cheeks scruffier around his normally, neatly trimmed goatee.

And he was still wearing my t-shirt.

"Goddam. I don't think I'll ever get tired of looking at you," I said, grabbing the material and pulling him to me in a kiss that he returned immediately. I sighed in relief, letting my tongue taste him as his hand snaked around the back of my neck. The kiss lingered and I let it go on. What the fuck did I care if he missed his plane?

The sound of murmurs and clapping broke through the moment and I groaned when he pulled away from me. I blinked, looking around at the crowd, waving at the guy taking my picture on his cellphone. He waved back and Etienne snorted with laughter as I turned back to face him.

"Want to tell me why you're here?" He asked, his fingers stroking my belly just above my waistline. His proximity to my cock was not helping my concentration. "Not that I minded having your tongue down my throat just before boarding. It was better than Starbucks."

I ignored his joke, diving in before I lost my nerve.

"I didn't come out to the whole world to play it safe. I spent years in the closet, passing up chances because I couldn't risk everything I'd worked so hard to get." I fisted my t-shirt again, pulling him close to look him in the eye as I took a leap and tried to keep my ass off somebody's couch one day. "But I got tired of living a half-life, of worrying about someone else controlling me because of the secrets I wrapped around my me. I was alone and afraid and sick and tired of living that way. When I stepped out on that stage at the press conference, I promised myself that I wouldn't live like that again."

He stared at me, his gaze kind but wary. "And what does that have to do with me?"

"It has *everything* to do with you," I said, grinning when his own face broke into a smile at my words. "I want to try this with you. Long distance sucks but I think I'd be very good at phone sex or Skype-sex. Whatever kind of sex." He wasn't stopping me so I just kept going, hoping that something would convince him to say yes. "And I can fly to NOLA all the time. Hockey season will be tricky but I don't play year-round and we can coordinate our schedules to make it work." I took a deep breath and went for it. "I don't want to be old and gray with old balls, lying in some home regretting the fact that I never figured out if what we have is real. I don't want to miss seeing you first thing in the morning, or missing you so damn much and being pissed because I can't see you every night. I just don't want to miss out on 'us'."

Etienne didn't say anything, just stared at me. I gave him his time, knowing he'd need to process everything I'd just said. It was a lot. It was fast.

He leaned into me, pressing our foreheads together and spoke just loudly enough for me to hear.

"I don't want to miss out on 'us' either." He laughed, pulling me into a tight hug and kissing along my jaw, my neck, ending right at my ear. "I want you, *cher*."

I closed my eyes, wrapping arms around his body and squeezing him tight to me. I was shaking. The big, mean professional hockey player was shaking. A bit of it was fear. A lot of it was excitement. Most of it was happiness.

Etienne pushed me back a step and I took advantage and kissed him again. This time it was full of heat but also something more. Nothing I could name but something I was looking forward to figuring out.

We broke apart and I glanced up at the clock. "I think you're going to miss your flight."

He grabbed my face and turned me back to look at him. Etienne gave me the crooked smile that I really hoped was just for me. "There's another one tomorrow morning at the ass-crack of dawn." He took my hand and pulled me towards the exit and a cab with our names on it. "We need to celebrate. You're not a free agent anymore."

I looked down at our hands, linked together. "No. I'm not."

DC

Three months later.
  Verizon Center, Washington DC.
Game day against the Cajun Rage

GAME DAY WAS ALWAYS EXCITING.

No matter what my intentions, I woke at the ass crack of dawn and the hours passed by at warp-speed and my skin got tighter and tighter on my frame with each passing hour. I relaxed, ate right, did some light exercise to warm up my muscles and tried to get into the right headspace to kick some ass for my team, my teammates, my city, and my fans. It's always a challenge, trying to temporarily cage the hulking beast rattling the prison bars and dying to bash some heads on the ice. Game day was always a long-ass day.

But everything slowed down the minute I got to the Verizon Center and started the long walk down the hall to the locker room. It's never quiet, but with my earbuds in and Mettalica assaulting my ears, my world finally slowed down. I usually got laser-focused on what needed to happen, how I would execute plays that I'd practiced over and over in my head and on the ice. No matter what happened outside this stadium, once I was there I knew this was what I was meant to do. I had tunnel vision.

But not today. Today my focus was on the man walking down the hall towards me.

Etienne. Looking sexy as shit, wearing the other team's jersey and a shit-eating grin that grew wider and sexier when I let out a low growl of disapproval.

Etienne's smile faltered when I grabbed his arm and dragged him into an empty office just to my right. I closed the door behind us, flipped the lock and turned on him with another feral growl. I crowded him, smiling a little when he hit the wall and I trapped him there with the weight of my body. He pressed back, moving against me as he parted his legs just wide enough for me to fill the spot reserved just for me. Nobody else. Just me.

"I know you work for them but I like it better when you wear my jersey," I said, nipping his earlobe before continuing across his jaw with kisses, relishing the rough-stubble rasp of it against my lips.

"I thought you liked it better when I wore nothing."

"No," I answered, pulling back to look at him. "I fucking *love* it."

Etienne's eyes did that thing where they morph into a molten, sexy, whiskey-colored pool that makes me hard and needy for him. This time was no different and I opened to him when he pressed his mouth on mine and wasted no time sweeping inside with his hot, wet tongue. I moaned and he wrapped is hand around my neck and held me in place, devouring my mouth. I dug my fingers into his hips, dragging our cocks together before sliding my hands to the front where I could cup his long, thick meat.

Two weeks. That's how long it had been since I'd seen him and we were both starving for it. For each other. It hadn't been easy but we'd made it work so far and we were both committed to seeing where it would go.

I stroked him through the fabric of his pants, loving the groan that forced him to break our kiss and bang his head against the wall behind him in frustration.

"We can't do this now," he forced out between panting breaths. He reached up to run his thumb along my lower lip and I licked it, tasting the salty sweet of his skin.

"I could suck you," I said.

He shook is head. "After two weeks all I want is to be buried inside your tight ass, *baby*. Nothing else is going to do it." His hand drifted down to my crotch and gave it a squeeze. "I could blow you. Take the edge off."

Etienne coated all of his words with the sexy-burr of his bayou upbringing and it almost broke my will. Almost.

"I don't get off before a game. It fucks with my mojo,"

"You still holding on to that superstition? You know that my Mamere will make the gris-gris for you."

I grinned, pressing a lazy kiss to his mouth. "I don't need your grandma's voodoo to keep my game-shit together. I got this." I kissed him again, happy to finally be in the same room with my man. I grinned and pulled our hips together in a final long, slow grind and owned the groan that pushed out from between his full lips. "I got you."

"Yeah, you do." His eyes turned hot and tender, his smile sweet. "I love you, Jamie."

I'd been the first one to say it and I never got tired of hearing him repeat those words to me. We were all in and it felt damn good.

"I love you too, *baby*," I said, giving my piss-poor imitation of his accent while I tugged on his jersey and gave it the most evil side-eye I could muster. "I don't like you wearing the uniform of the enemy even if they do give you a paycheck with a job which fulfills all your dreams and shit."

He grinned, raising an eyebrow as he unfastened his belt, the top button and slid down the zipper on his fly.

"I thought we just covered that we weren't going to polish our knobs right now."

"Just shut up," he smirked as he pulled down his pants and turned showing off his fine ass in boxer briefs in my team colors. They had the team logo sitting on the juiciest part of his left cheek.

And my jersey number emblazoned on the right.

"You bought a pair?" I laughed. The marketing arm of the team had cashed in on the gay fans who showed up at our games with my number on their jerseys and offered up the men's underwear for them. My teammates had given me never-ending shit about it every time a fan asked me to autograph a pair after a game. I did it with a grin on my face and a well-aimed middle finger aimed in their direction.

But they looked fucking amazing on Etienne.

"I did," he said, pulling up and zipping his pants. "No matter what happens on the ice tonight. You're my man and I'm rooting for you every time. That being said, the Rage is going to wipe the ice with ya'll." Once he was all tucked in, he leaned in to give me a kiss full of humor and a little heat when his tongue swiped along my lower lip. "Winner's choice in bed tonight."

Another kiss, this one from me, fiercer with a hint of teeth and a growl. "We're going to kick your ass."

"Really? You want to get lucky and that's what you say to me?" He smiled, the one that's just for me that says he's got it as bad for me as I do for him.

He slid past me and I let him because I needed to get to the locker room to actually do my job. But I got in the parting shot.

"I'm already lucky."

THE END

A LETTER TO YOU, DEAR READER

Dear Reader —

Thanks so much for reading my book. If you enjoyed reading about these stories you can find out latest info on my next release and enter for the monthly giveaway by signing up for my newsletter:

NEWSLETTER SIGNUP: http://bit.ly/1hde9GD

And if you are so inclined, please leave a review on Amazon, Barnes & Noble, iBooks, or Goodreads.

I love to explore the theme of fooling around and falling in love in my books and I adore a hero who falls hard. When I'm not writing sexy, sizzling romance, I collect tasty man candy pics, indulge in a little comic book geek love, collect red nail polish, spoil my Corgi (the one and only, Dixie Joan Wilder!) and obsess over Chris Evans. Drop me a line at robin@robin-covingtonrmance.com and tell me what you obsess over!

Xx,
    Robin

SOCIAL MEDIA LINKS

Social Media Links:

Email: robin@robincovingtonromance.com
　　Website: http://bit.ly/1lewhMg
　　Facebook Profile: http://on.fb.me/YSW9n3
　　Facebook Page: http://on.fb.me/1fCyWuQ
　　Twitter: @RobinCovington
　　Tumblr: http://robincovingtonromance.tumblr.com
　　Instagram: https://instagram.com/robincovington/
　　Pinterest: http://bit.ly/1c1Tm5u
　　Amazon Follow: http://amzn.to/1L2PrAG
　　Street Team: http://on.fb.me/1hZdeEu
　　Newsletter sign up: http://bit.ly/1hde9GD

OTHER BOOKS BY ROBIN COVINGTON

If you enjoyed TAKING CHANCES, check out my other books:

A NIGHT OF SOUTHERN COMFORT
 HIS SOUTHERN TEMPTATION
 SWEET SOUTHERN BETRAYAL
 SOUTHERN NIGHTS AND SECRETS
 PLAYING THE PART
 SEX & THE SINGLE VAMP
 PLAYING WITH THE DRUMMER
 DARING THE PLAYER
 TEMPTATION
 SALVATION
 REDEMPTION
 THE PRINCE'S RUNAWAY LOVER
 ONE LITTLE KISS
 SECRET SANTA BABY
 RUSH
 SHADOW RANCH

WHEN YOU OPEN YOUR EYES
SLEEPING WITH THE ENEMY
SEXY SECOND CHANCES